PICTURING THE WRECK

Dani Shapiro

A PLUME BOOK

PLUME
Published by the Penguin Group
Penguin Books USA Inc., 375 Hudson Street, New York, New York 10014, U.S.A.
Penguin Books Ltd, 27 Wrights Lane, London W8 5TZ, England
Penguin Books Australia Ltd, Ringwood, Victoria, Australia
Penguin Books Canada Ltd, 10 Alcorn Avenue, Toronto, Ontario, Canada M4V 3B2
Penguin Books (N.Z.) Ltd, 182–190 Wairau Road, Auckland 10, New Zealand

Penguin Books Ltd, Registered Offices: Harmondsworth, Middlesex, England

Published by Plume, an imprint of Dutton Signet,
a division of Penguin Books USA Inc.
This is an authorized reprint of a hardcover edition published by Doubleday,
a division of Bantam Doubleday Dell Publishing Group, Inc.
For information address Bantam Doubleday Dell Publishing Group, Inc.,
1540 Broadway, New York, NY 10036.

First Plume Printing, February, 1997
10 9 8 7 6 5 4 3 2 1

Ⓟ REGISTERED TRADEMARK—MARCA REGISTRADA

CIP data is available.

Printed in the United States of America
Original hardcover design by Jennifer Ann Daddio

PUBLISHER'S NOTE
This is a work of fiction. Names, characters, places, and incidents either are the
products of the author's imagination or are used fictitiously, and any resemblance
to actual persons, living or dead, events, or locales is entirely coincidental.

This book is for my family—
my mother, Irene,
my sister, Sue,
and for Craig.

ACKNOWLEDGMENTS

I WOULD PARTICULARLY LIKE TO THANK Helen Schulman and Mary Morris for their insightful comments on early drafts.

David Hoopes of the State Department and Patrick Bradley of the United States Department of Justice were very generous with their time and expertise.

For their moral support: Hallie Gay Walden Bagley, Elizabeth Fagan, Penny and Marvin Bromberg, Rollene Saal, and Jennifer Wolff.

Deb Futter and Esther Newberg are, quite simply, the best.

And lastly, my abiding gratitude to a man who did not live long enough to see himself thanked: Jerome Badanes— novelist, teacher, mentor, dear friend.

Sin is a dangerous toy in the
hands of the virtuous. It should
be left to the congenitally sinful,
who know when to play with it,
and when to let it alone.

—H. L. MENCKEN

PROLOGUE

YOUR EYES ARE a deep, milky blue—the color of the September 1
dusk, the color of the blanket your mother has wrapped around you as
tightly as a coccoon. You squirm and fidget. Is it a game she is
playing? You screech as she rushes, holding you with one arm, care-
less, slamming doors, tripping on the fringe of the Persian rug. You
gurgle with delight as she almost drops you on your downy head—
"almost" is not a word in your vocabulary. Yours is the black-and-
white world of infancy.

You do not see the sliver of yellow, the bright man-made lemony
taxicab waiting by the curb as she throws her jacket over her shoul-
ders, then hurls her house keys at me. You hear the silence of the late-
summer night, the click of your mother's heels as she makes her way
down the front steps. No one says a word. You playfully reach out for
me—you don't know how to say "Daddy"—as I grab onto whatever I
can: the sleeve of her jacket, a hunk of her hair, then finally the blue
blanket. I hold onto the blanket's edge, my fist as tightly closed and

stubborn as a child's. Ruthie stares at me, her dark eyes like twin closed doors, then pulls you out of the blanket, leaving it to unfurl in my outstretched hand.

She carries no suitcase, though she will never return. You are her only luggage, all she will ever need in this world. She shoves me aside with more force than I would have thought possible, her delicate little chin preceding her as she moves past me, shielding you with her whole body. As the taxi door slams, I am left holding a still-warm blue blanket, the corner carefully sewn with a name tag: Daniel Grossman.

I hold the thin fabric to my nose and inhale deeply, committing your talcum powder and baby sweat to memory. I have behaved like an animal, and now I have lost you in the wilderness. But animals can always sniff out their young. I will live my life with my nose to the ground. I will hold you in my lungs. No matter how many years it takes, some day I will track your footprints through the forest.

ONE

THIS MORNING BEGINS like all other mornings. I awaken at
six forty-eight to National Public Radio, which serves its purpose, instantly erasing my dreams. I lie in bed, staring at the
ceiling, listening to the sounds below. Already, the city is
humming with life. On the other side of my brownstone door,
bleary-eyed men walk their dogs, jog in Riverside Park, hail
cabs on their way to breakfast meetings. In a few hours there
will be the sound of jackhammers in the distance erecting a
high-rise on Broadway, and Riverside Drive will be filled
with flocks of young mothers walking their children to nursery school. As for myself, like any other day, I will not stray
far from home until it is dark.

I shave in the shower, then pad through the steamy
bathroom like a ghost, leaving wet footprints on the pale blue
bedroom carpet. Boxer shorts, suit, tie. Always the same. The

house faintly buzzes with silence. I try to drown it with the radio, but I hear silence in the spaces between words.

I walk downstairs, turn on the television in the kitchen, and see blankness in the flat gray eyes of this morning's harbinger of death and destruction. I marvel at my powers of repression: I hear the snap, crackle, pop of my cereal more clearly than "Good Morning America." After all, who can listen to the latest and go on with his day? My kitchen is filled with instruments of self-destruction: oven, microwave, corkscrew, freshly sharpened knives. Objects which take on a life of their own. Objects which plead with me, beg me in the silence.

Of course my patients think I have answers for them. They dream of knives, of dark tunnels, and the glint of white teeth, the flash of gold fillings. Gardens more ornate than Versailles, worms curling around the roots of trees. They tell me their dreams and secrets. They believe they are telling me the truth, but usually the truth is buried deep within their version of it. They look at me with the wide, guileless eyes of infants. They should only know their doctor sits in his kitchen watching the news, listening to the melody of NPR and the polyrhythmic pops from his bowl of Rice Krispies until the print of the *New York Times* rearranges itself in a bark of degradation. And the knives begin to dance. The handles beckon. The oven door throws out a welcome mat. My seven-thirty patient should only know how often, simply by showing up on time, he has saved his doctor's life.

The early news has a cute redheaded newscaster these days. An Irish girl. Usually I keep her on mute. The officious, marble-mouthed vowels she affects ruin the picture. But this morning it isn't the redhead who catches my attention, but rather, the footage of a plane crash behind her. Pieces of a jet, cockpit broken like a prehistoric egg, helicopters hovering. Firefighters in black-and-yellow slickers spraying hoses the width of men, bodies piled on the tarmac. It is human nature to be fascinated by the terrible, even as we shade our eyes from it. Think of that awful tradition the goyim have, the wake. If there's a dead body in the room, it is impossible not to gawk.

I turn up the volume. The redhead gazes deeply into the eyes of America.

Good morning. All one hundred and thirty-eight people on board World Air 103, a 737 bound for Cleveland, are presumed dead after last night's devastating crash at Los Angeles International Airport.

5

I am well acquainted with bodies piled like garbage. I grope for the remote, hoping to switch the channel to something cheerier—Bugs Bunny, or Regis Philbin, perhaps. Any day that begins with images of mass destruction can go nowhere but downhill. But then, the redhead throws me a curveball.

And here to speak with us is Daniel Gross from the National Transportation Safety Board.

What if I hadn't seen his face or heard the name? If I had switched the channel just a second sooner, or kept the redhead on mute? If life had moved a fraction sideways, things would now be different. Or more aptly, they would be exactly the same: the dirge of National Public Radio, a breakfast of Rice Krispies and buttered toast, eight hours of patients, then a twilight walk down Riverside Drive to the Seventy-ninth Street boat basin and back, a microwave dinner.

There is a kind of nobility in the solitary way I have lived most of my life. At times I have felt like a lab rat in an experiment of my own making: Can a man survive with no woman? no son? no reputation? no love? But this morning my past has fallen from its dusty shelf. *Here now, live in Los Angeles, is Daniel Gross, from the National Transportation Safety Board.* So she shortened his name. Eliminated the "man." Sliced me away like a malignant growth. Did she think I'd just disappear? Bow my head and slink off into the underbrush? Life has a way of evening the score, if only we are patient.

6

I PACK MY BAGS without a moment's hesitation, and with great authority, as if jumping onto airplanes is something I do on a regular basis. Two shirts, herringbone jacket, cashmere cardigan, gray flannel trousers, a small pile of undershirts, four pairs of black socks, four boxers. Dopp kit: shaving cream, disposable razor, travel-sized toothbrush and toothpaste courtesy of Air France circa 1970, mint-flavored floss, fancy pastille tin which actually contains codeine, Tylenol, Valium, doxycycline—the Jewish man's idea of a survival kit for the wilderness of Southern California.

At the bottom of the dopp kit, where other men might hide their condoms, is a yellowed clipping, decades old. I had almost forgotten it was there. I carefully unfold it, paper so stiff it may disintegrate at any moment. The clipping and I have aged at about the same rate. I am stiff and yellowed, my skin papery and ready to crumble if touched. But the subject of the clipping has not aged a day: a single black braid snakes down her back, and her pale blue eyes gaze calmly at the camera. This is the definitive photograph of Katrina Volk, though it is not the one I carry in my mind. In the almost-gaunt hollows beneath her Germanic cheekbones, the stillness of her body, her long legs folded beneath her, she seems like a beast, an exotic creature best observed from a distance, behind bars, beneath glass. At the same time she begs you, she dares you. *Touch me.*

I check my watch. Ten minutes before my first patient arrives. I lie back on the bed, the bedspread bunched beneath me, cream-colored crochet, coarse against my skin as I push my pants around my ankles. No time to remove socks or shoes, nor any inclination. My feet dangle off the bed, and somehow this indignity only furthers my excitement. I balance the clipping of Katrina on my stomach, my erection rising between my pale thighs like a volcanic formation, a strange sight protruding from the gray pinstripes and starched white shirt surrounding it. Not bad for a sixty-four-year-old man. A pity there's no one here to witness me in all my glory. In the clipping, Katrina is crouched against the pebbled concrete outside a New York City tenement. She is wearing khaki pants, and if I squint I can make out her vulva against the soft tan cloth. A Leica hangs around her neck, a case of lenses is slung over her shoulder.

For the first time in many years, my body craves Katrina

Volk. A sexual syrup has soaked into my brain like booze, numbing me as I stroke myself. Her camera, khakis, nails bitten to the quick—I am flooded with details I have spent three decades trying to forget. It is possible that my memory has bestowed upon Katrina a near-mythological status. In my mind's eye she is forever twenty-four, as lithe and beautiful as she was the year she darkened my office door. I close my eyes and try to imagine her as she must be today: a middle-aged woman. Would she have aged gracefully? Would she have gotten the face she deserved?

I open my eyes and conjure Katrina at the foot of my bed. Her body has grown fuller with age, her face creased and handsome. Her hair has sprung loose from its usual single braid. It cascades over her shoulders, stiff pink nipples peeking at me from beneath dark waves. She opens her mouth—I am afraid she is going to speak—but instead she bends over, breasts swaying. My lonely hand is replaced by her lips as she moves rhythmically, swallowing me up.

I'm going to see my son, Katrina.

If you live long enough, you always get a second chance.

MY SEVEN-THIRTY ARRIVES one minute late, huffing in sweatpants and hooded jacket. I usher him into my office. He sits on the edge of the couch, jiggling his leg—my favorite overachiever who crams psychoanalysis into a jam-packed morning of triathalon training while listening to books-on-tape. He looks edgily around the room, as if he hasn't seen it a thousand times before: venetian blinds tilted against the light, shelves crammed with psychoanalytic tomes, desk strewn with pamphlets and half-finished correspondence, a small digital clock blinking each of his precious fifty minutes away. The floor is covered by a threadbare oriental. My walls are devoid of art. Two framed letters, the correspondence between Freud and Ferenczi, hang above the radiator.

I lean back in my chair and fold my hands over my stomach. Jeffrey, my seven-thirty, is almost exactly the same age as my son. I seem to treat a great number of young men. Each day I shine a flashlight into the dark corners of early adulthood and wonder which particular set of problems has plagued Daniel. One thing is certain: he has not escaped unscathed. He is the product of a mother who abducted him, a father he has never known. Perhaps he bolts awake in the hours before dawn, the whites of his eyes fear-shaped crescents in the dark of his room. His breath strangles him and he lets out a scream and whoever shares his bed shakes him awake, soothes him with the universal words: *darling, it was just a dream.*

"It happened again last night," Jeffrey begins.

On the cusp of marriage to the perfect woman, Jeffrey wants to know why he's experiencing clinical panic attacks on bridges, in tunnels, while making love to his future bride.

I nod, but say nothing.

"I thought I was having a heart attack. Sweating palms, tinging fingers, pain in my chest—"

"What do you think is going on?" I ask.

"Maybe I should see a cardiologist—it's not unheard of, you know—"

"So you still think these problems are organic?" I mildly respond. He has had three complete physicals in the past six months.

Jeffrey glares at me from across the room. (This one refuses the couch.)

"What do *you* think is going on, Dr. Grossman?"

I don't want to respond. He has to figure out for himself that you can't build a frame around your life, wrap it with a red satin ribbon, and call it a day.

"How's Martha?" I ask, suggesting a different place for those broken fears of his.

My concentration is shaky. As I listen to Jeffrey extol the virtues of Martha (much as I might have praised Ruthie to the high heavens thirty-odd years ago) my mind wanders west to Los Angeles. How powerful are the genetic strands linking me to my son? Sometimes when I close my eyes I see tiny, amoeba-shaped cells floating beneath my lids. Or I imagine the milky fluid of my ejaculate filled with spermatazoa swimming madly, blindly, to the dead end of the small puddle near my belly button.

It is possible that my son has an intense interest in psychoanalysis, that he abhors pickled herring, is allergic to walnuts, partial to Brahms. He may drum his fingers quietly against one knee as I am doing now, much to the consternation of young Jeffrey. He may be neither a leg nor a breast man, but rather, be overwhelmed by a graceful neck, a narrow waist, a high, intelligent forehead.

In twenty-four hours I will have the answers to a lifetime of questions. My plane will touch down at LAX and my rental car will be waiting.

Poor Jeffrey Sawyer, and the rest of my Monday patients. Their usual Dr. Grossman is not in attendance, but merely his shadow. I remember a professor who once told me that the best class he had ever taught was the one he had missed. Perhaps my patients will heal themselves, just this once.

"Mr. Sawyer, I will be gone for the rest of the week, so I won't be able to meet you at our usual Thursday hour," I say.

He looks startled. Rarely do our sessions end with any words other than my usual, gently invoked *Our time is up.*

"A family crisis," I volunteer.

Why am I telling him this? God knows what he'll project onto me with this information.

"I'm sorry," he says, standing and stretching his long, runner's legs. "So I'll see you next Monday?"

"If I'm delayed I'll have my secretary call you."

"And if I have another attack?"

"You will survive the fear, Mr. Sawyer."

He extends a hand to me, and as I grasp his damp palm I see a flicker behind his eyes, a light which brightens, then dims. "Right," he says. A revelation.

As soon as the door clicks shut, I pick up the phone, dial directory assistance in Washington, and ask the operator for Daniel Gross. She has no Daniels, but three initial D's. I ask her for all three numbers, and scribble them on a yellow legal pad. It has been many years since I've looked for my son. When he was a boy, I always knew where he was. I hired detectives, kept tabs on him from a distance. But as he grew older, knowing became more painful than not knowing. Until today, when I saw his face and finally had no choice in the matter.

An answering machine picks up on the first ring. "Hi, it's Darlene. Let me know who *you* are, and I'll call ya right back." I listen for a moment to the chirpy voice followed by a long beep, feeling a familiar pang of missed opportunity.

I dial again. ". . . I'm sorry, but the number you have dialed, (202) 555-0584, has been disconnected. No further information is available about (202) 555—"

The recorded voice sounds vaguely put out, as if I should have known better.

Two down, one to go. There is a slight tremor in my fingers. I've never quite adjusted to push buttons; my fingers still long for the old-fashioned dial, the tactile arc, each hole just fitting the tip of my index finger.

My heart skips a beat when I hear a man's voice answer the phone.

"Hello?" he says.

"Hello," I croak. "I'm sorry, is this—"

". . . this is Dan. I'm not available to take your call, but if you leave a message, I'll get back to you."

I hang up and dial again. The ten digits in front of me have all the significance of a code it has taken me three decades to crack. *Hello, this is Dan.* The voice is deep, slightly hoarse. Maybe he smokes. He has a cigarettes-and-whiskey voice. *I'm not available to take your call.* Available. The word is as round as a marble in my mouth. My son calls himself Dan. He works for the government. He lives in Washington, D.C., and is investigating a plane crash in Los Angeles. His voice has rough edges to it.

. . . *leave a message, I'll get back to you.*

No, my ghost-child. It is I who will be getting back to you.

TWO

FOR THIRTY YEARS, I have lived with my ghosts. The photograph of Ruthie walking down the aisle on our wedding day still hangs above the dresser. The frame is slightly crooked. Watching me jerk off to the clipping of Katrina must have set her askew. She looks splendid, glowing the way girls did in the 1950s, stepping confidently down the aisle on the arm of her father, Meyer Lenski, Manhattan's first Jewish district attorney, and only one vowel away from Meyer Lansky, the great Jewish mafioso. Those white satin shoes transported her directly to the pathetic whimpering of our marital vows.

Although a maid comes in once a week to redistribute the dust, nothing much has changed since the day Ruthie's movers arrived and carted away a few pieces of furniture and much of the nursery. After the divorce, when I convinced the bank to let me buy the brownstone, in effect I bought the retention of my own memory. I have left the artifacts of my past intact, living with them like a tourist mistakenly trapped overnight in a wax museum—but the guards have never come, the doors have never opened. The night has gone on forever.

Ruthie began her quest for motherhood on our wedding night. We had been intimate prior to our marriage, but that evening, in the penthouse suite of the Hotel Pierre, Ruthie crumpled the little foil packet I pulled from my dopp kit, and tossed it across the room where it landed on the plush carpet next to an after-dinner-mint wrapper.

"We won't need these anymore," she whispered.

"But, Ruthie!" I protested. "We can't afford to take any chances!"

"I want to make a baby."

"I thought we agreed to wait."

"I don't want to wait," she said, her voice muffled between my thighs. Where had she learned such skill? I was her first, she told me. Was there a class wedged between gymnastics and comparative literature at the Dalton School—Blow-Jobs 101, perhaps? Did some cute teacher get up in front of the classroom and demonstrate on a banana?

Ruthie climbed on top of me and began to gyrate like a pro. She was still wearing her brassiere, a lacy, push-up affair, her breasts raised in a gravity-defying cleavage that nearly made me spill into her on the spot.

"Slow down, I want it to last," I murmured, but she was lost to the world. She leaned down and brushed the stiff lace of her bra against my cheeks. I was bursting with love for my brand-new wife, who was as lush and opulent as the silk tapestries lining the walls of our suite.

Her nipples were darkened, so stiff they pushed out from beneath the demi-cups of her bra. Back and forth, back and forth. Was this another course they offered at the famed Dalton School? No wonder it was such a popular place. How did the girls learn the art of seduction? Did they practice on each other? Another delicious thought—with which I exploded.

Desire turned instantly into abject terror.

"Ruthie, that was stupid," I said.

"Mmmm," she murmured into my damp chest.

"No, really. We shouldn't have done that."

"You didn't like it?" Her eyes blinked up at me, innocent, flirtatious.

"Of course I did. That's not the—"

"Husband," she interrupted.

"Sorry?"

"My husband," she said, and the fear subsided. With one possessive pronoun she had cut right to the heart of me. It had been many years since I had belonged to anyone. Ruthie was now my only living relative.

"We can't afford a baby yet," I whispered gently.

She sat up in the bed.

"Can't afford?" she snapped. "What's 'can't afford'? You have to get over this poverty mentality, Solomon."

"But I *am* poor."

"*We're* not. We have all the money we need."

"Your parents' money," I said flatly.

"Yes, so what?"

"You've never done a single thing to earn that money, Ruthie," I began. "What makes it so easy for you to—"

"How dare you!"

I fell silent.

"How dare you tell me how to live! You don't seem to mind Mama and Daddy buying us a brownstone," she yelled so loudly I was worried the other hotel guests might complain.

"That's different."

"How? How is it different?"

My new wife's cheeks were flushed from the one-two punch of sex and rage.

"Ruthie, I just want to make it on our own."

"How stupid, Solomon."

Had she ever been denied anything? I wondered. She had never heard those two little words: *can't afford.* That night, as I fell asleep, I prayed to my sperm, now swimming inside Ruthie: *Go the other way, buddy. Swim out, not in.*

Given time, I believed Ruthie would eventually understand my need to build a family without her parents' largesse. I would gratefully accept a house, a brand-new Maytag dishwasher, a sterling silver mezzuzah—I saw all that as the foundation for my new, perfect family. But my very sense of manhood depended on my ability to forge, from the ground up, that which the war had stolen from me.

As it happened, my sperm listened to me that night and for many nights to follow. They fought harder against Ruthie than I did. After a while, I gave in. But my body had a mind of its own. A baby was the first thing Ruth Lenski Grossman ever asked for that she didn't get *tout de suite.* And this is how the first years of my marriage—the only years, as it turned out —came to be spent shuttling from doctor to infertility specialist to hospital. *Daniel, how we wanted you.* My son was injected into his mama with such force that my sperm had no choice but to cling to the walls and hold on.

MY WEDDING DAY was the last innocent day of my life. As I slid the ring onto Ruthie's finger, I believed there were no social barriers, no class structure, no *us* versus *them.* Character was something you built. The mere fact of surviving, of escaping the war, had given me the courage to invent a new self from whole cloth. And perhaps I was even better this way, stronger for having emerged from the clouds of my imagination than from the bowels of history.

And yet, looking around me, I could not help but feel that the pendulum of my life had swung from the Rykestrasse in Berlin to the elegant, stained-glass interior of the wealthiest shul in New York City in startlingly quick time. The Park Avenue Synagogue was very prettily divided into two distinct sections: bouquets of cream-colored roses and loops of white satin ribbon separating the bride's side from the groom's.

I had certainly married well. Behind the Lenski clan, there were two senators, a Supreme Court justice, and Fiorello La Guardia in the second row. On my side of the aisle, in the pews where my family would have sat, were friends and professors from my doctoral program, awkward in their tweed jackets and stained ties.

For an instant, as I took in the chasm between our families, a little voice in my head told me to escape. I imagined dashing up the aisle past Ruthie, her father, and our four hundred guests, and hailing a cab on the corner of Park and Eighty-seventh. Where to? the driver would ask. And what would I say? Where would I go? I had no family to speak of. My parents had escaped the war to live in an undistinguished high-rise where they watched television all day long until they died one after the other, while I was in college. The rest of my relatives had been killed in the camps. There was nowhere to go. Everyone I even marginally cared about in the world was seated in the ornate splendor of the Park Avenue Synagogue.

By the time I heard the first strains of Mendelssohn's Wedding March, I realized I had utterly, completely committed myself. I looked at the faces of my City College pals, for whom Mama Lenski had graciously rented tuxedos, and swallowed hard, amazed at the distance I had traveled.

Ruthie's dark eyes shone as she wafted toward me in an ivory silk cloud. She believed I was her deliverance. We had known each other precisely three months, since she had attended an open symposium at the Institute. I was blinded by the delicate sheen of her beauty, a loveliness burnished by the finest Madison Avenue salons. The bottoms of her feet were as soft as the curve of her cheek. I had never before met anyone who had not suffered. My life was filled with survivors and doctoral students. No one becomes a psychoanalyst because they've had an easy time of it. I suppose I thought I could borrow some of Ruthie's ease, tack it over my own wounds like a bandage. Now we would be joined together, like our names on the contract with which we purchased (with her father's money) the brownstone on Eighty-ninth and Riverside. We would be like a law firm: Lenski & Grossman. Ruthie was one of the first women to hyphenate; she wasn't going to give up Daddy's name for some poor shnook of a graduate student. She was smart enough to know she had lived a sheltered life. I was experience, history, suffering: her form of rebellion. I dare say she got more than she bargained for.

THAT WAS MY FIRST MISTAKE. Marrying your mother. Sometimes at night, when I can't fall asleep, I count mistakes instead of sheep. This is the house of cards which turned out to be my life: If I hadn't married Ruthie, then we never would have bought the brownstone, then I wouldn't have had my practice on Riverside and Eighty-ninth, then Katrina Volk would never have walked into my life.

I wouldn't have had you. But then again—I wouldn't have lost you.

EVERY DAY, for as long as I can remember, I have taken my lunch in Riverside Park, weather permitting. This is my daily meal: bologna and mustard on rye, unsweetened iced tea, an apple cinnamon cookie from the baker on the corner of Eighty-ninth and Broadway. I sit on the same park bench, just north of the slope which leads down to the Hudson River. The park has its own rhythm: a young woman walks a pack of neighborhood dogs each day, leashes extended from her thin wrist like the strings of a parachute. Nannies walk strollers down to the promenade, around the ornate fence of the community flower garden and back up to the elegant doorman buildings on Riverside and West End. There is a yeshiva on the corner which sometimes allows its boys a study break, and they swarm like black-and-white dalmatians down the slope, squinting, skin pale in the sunlight, black curls flying, rumpled white shirts half-tucked into black trousers, white socks, black shoes—the only color in sight the blotchy red skin of adolescence.

My last memory of my son is on this hill. It was a Friday night, the twenty-first of February, and I found a brand-new sled perched against a garbage can on West End Avenue as I walked home from analytic supervision. The sled was in perfect condition: burnished wood, small red blades, an anchor-shaped handle which steered the front blades from side to side. I wondered why it had been abandoned.

When I walked through the front door, Ruthie took one look at me and rolled her eyes.

"No, absolutely not," she protested, even as I bundled her into her coat, wrapped Daniel, already in his Dr. Denton's, in a snowsuit and small quilt, and pulled them across the street with me.

There had been a blizzard that afternoon, and the slope was covered with virgin snow. The park was empty. In those days it was safe. There were no broken vials of drugs on the pavement, no beer bottles wedged into snowbanks. No danger lurked behind the bushes and shrubs. Shadows did not make you jump and scream. My wife, son, and I walked to the top of the hill and looked through the bare branches at the sporadic lights of New Jersey winking across the river. Daniel clung to me, fists around my neck, knees against my stomach, breath tickling my jaw, and my whole body ached with love for him.

"Stay here," I told Ruthie.

"Solomon, no!"

"It's perfectly safe," I said as I eased myself onto the sled. I turned Daniel around so we were both facing the slope, crossed my arms over his chest, stuck my feet on the sled's rudders and pushed off.

As we zigzagged down the hill, wearing our matching knitted caps, I thought we must look rather dashing, like an advertisement straight from the pages of the *Saturday Evening Post*. "Father and child cutting a swath through the thin February air."

My son started screaming before I did. I like to think his eyes were closed, that he was shrieking with joy, but more likely he saw the slate gray rock rising like an island from the whiteness and felt the thud in the instant before our sled flipped over and we rolled onto the icy pathway leading down to the pavement. I held him as the blade of the sled cleared his head by less than an inch, cupping him against my chest, shielding him with my body as Ruth's howl came closer and closer, like the wail of an ambulance. With Daniel safe in my arms, I panted thanks to God before Ruthie snatched him from me and ran back up the hill, leaving me behind.

I lay on the ground, not even feeling the wet snow seeping through my woolen jacket. Daniel's cap had fallen only inches from my hand, but I was afraid to move. My back was numb, and I couldn't feel my legs. I thought of the snow-angels I used to make as a child, jumping from rooftops into freshly fallen snow, arms and legs flung wide. I have few early childhood memories from the years before my family fled the war, but I remember the sky on those early winter nights—the wide, indifferent German sky. I knew, once we left for America, that my friends still in Germany were living under a darker sky, thrown over them like a pitch-black blanket.

I wanted to give my son those stars. I wanted him to feel the speed of life as we barreled down that hill—boldness knitted into his young bones. I wanted to drench his brain with courage. I knew this about the human psyche: it is shaped during the first few years of life, then hardened and glazed. If timidity and self-doubt are molded into the soft tissue, they will stay there forever. I had been born feeling the foreshocks of annihilation. I was determined that Daniel know no fear.

Instead I had damaged him (not physically, thank God, the blades only skimmed the top of his downy head like a lawnmower over soft summer grass), hand-delivered a psychic wound which would stay with him always, whether or not he consciously remembered it. Many years later, on an analyst's couch, Daniel might present a puzzling dream: black rock, virgin snow, arms lifting him from danger. *Whose arms?* the analyst would want to know. (I myself would certainly probe in that direction.) *Whose arms made you feel safe?*

Although it could not have been more than a few minutes, it seemed an hour before I crept back up the slope and crossed Riverside Drive. My back was sore and the ground felt less solid than it had moments earlier. A lone Checker skidded to a stop in front of my house, and Bernie Appelbaum, Daniel's pediatrician, emerged from its mud-stained yellow door. Doctors still made house calls in those days, arriving with their mysterious small black bags. (I have always envied those bags. The tools of my trade do not have a shape, they do not hang impressively around my neck and glisten.) Bernie gave me a halfhearted wave when he saw me hobbling across the street. I'm sure he didn't relish being dragged to the West Side at dinnertime by a hysterical mother. His chin was buried in his muffler, but it was so bitter cold his breath escaped through the woolen knit in a cloud.

"Solomon." He stuck out his hand.

"That was fast," I said, grasping it more firmly than was reasonable.

"What happened?"

"I honestly can't tell you, Bernie. Minor accident. Everything's okay."

I was deflated, winded. I could hear the shakiness in my own voice.

"Well, Ruth sounded utterly frantic," he said in a doctorly voice I knew was reserved only for men who had witnessed marital warfare: clubby and covert, but absolutely neutral—*you're on your own, buddy.*

Appelbaum shifted his weight back and forth as I fumbled through my pockets for keys. My pants were soaked, and my body shook with an involuntary chill.

"We'd better get inside before *you* become the patient," he said heartily, slapping the sides of his overcoat. His nose, poking over the top of his scarf, was bright red.

"Locked out," I smiled feebly. I was sure he was wondering what I had been doing in Riverside Park in the first place. I rang the doorbell of my own house. I heard the chimes (G and E, repeated twice—a piece of musical trivia I would not have known if not for my wife's perfect pitch) and the mouselike *rat-tat-tat* of Ruth's heels scurrying down the wooden staircase.

She flung the door open.

"Bernie, thank God."

My wife might have been a peasant woman had she been born in another time and place. I can picture her keening over an open grave, or tilling the fields with her rough peasant hands, or gathering a child to her sagging, empty breast. Timing and destiny are all that separate her from her ancestors, who lived in some long-forgotten Russian village. Ruth Lenski Grossman, daughter of the great Meyer, has manicured hands and smooth skin, courtesy of facials since age sixteen—but her common heart beats like the call of a drum.

She did not even look at me. She was holding Daniel against her hip, and his milky blue eyes were wide open, staring at us.

"What seems to be the matter—"

"He's—"

"Ruthie, nothing happened!" I interrupted. "He wasn't even—"

"Don't. Talk. To. Me." In the spaces between each word I saw an abyss, felt myself free-falling. In the world according to Ruth Lenski Grossman, I had done the one unforgivable thing: I had imperiled our son.

"Let's take a look at him," Appelbaum said, hoisting Daniel from Ruthie's arms and gently laying him down on the dining room table. Daniel was not much bigger than a placemat in those days. Appelbaum leaned his black doctor's bag against a silver candlestick, opened it like an accordion, and pulled out the instruments of his trade: stethoscope, bright pinpoint light, reflex hammer, a few ominous-looking syringes. Daniel began to shriek.

I heard Ruth moan behind me. I reached out for her and she cringed. This was to be expected. Ruth had been shrinking from me ever since Daniel's birth. (This is not an excuse. Only a fact. It sheds no light on my subsequent behavior. Morality, in my opinion, is not circumstantial. A man who has such an appetite will bite into the soft young flesh of forbidden fruit whether or not his wife opens her legs for him.) In the beginning, Ruth evicted me from our bed, pleading soreness, turning instead to an omnipresent stack of parenting books and magazines. She curled up with their hard edges like a lover. I slept on the living room sofa with a pillow and an afghan, relishing, I must admit, my discontent. This is what happens to men who follow the path of least resistance, I thought to myself as I stared at the living room walls, the piano covered with framed photographs of the Lenski clan. (I myself have exactly four photographs which survived the war. While the Lenskis were building their empire, my few remaining kin were vomiting their way across the Atlantic.) I had a doctorate, good standing at the Institute, a private practice, and the closest to a royal marriage a Jew could ever hope for—and I here was, lying alone on the elegant couch (teal blue crushed velvet) in my handsome living room (sixteen-foot oriental, antique Chinese porcelain resting on the marble coffee table so close my foot could kick it in my sleep), while my wife slept surrounded by Dr. Spock in the bedroom upstairs. *Who's the fool, Grossman,* a voice whispered nightly, serenading me, torturing me to sleep. *For this the bones of your aunts and uncles float in the Pond of Ashes?*

"Nothing seems to be wrong," Appelbaum said, peering with a light into Daniel's pupils. "I'd keep an eye on him over the next couple of days, see if anything develops."

"Develop? What could develop?" Ruth's words shimmied across the room. She had cornered the market on fear, that wife of mine. She had bought up the whole supply with her family's endless cash.

"He *didn't* hit his head," I muttered.

Bernie, bless his heart, flashed me a men-of-the-world-unite-against-hysterical-women wink.

"I'll bet you two haven't even had your dinner yet," he said. "Look, Ruth, why don't you have a glass of wine? Put your baby to bed and let Sol watch the Knicks on the telly. I think they're on at eight. Speaking of which—" He looked at his watch.

The door clicked shut behind the good doctor, leaving my little Molotov cocktail of a family intact. Ruth spun on her heel (I had never understood this expression until I met my wife, who wore neat Belgian shoes, expressly suited, it seemed, for such a purpose) and headed upstairs with Daniel.

I walked into the kitchen. I rarely drank, but the time seemed right for a shot of schnapps. I still hadn't changed and was chilled to the bone. We kept our liquor in a cabinet beneath the sink, according it the same importance as laundry detergent. There was a bottle of scotch down there, some slivovitz and several dusty bottles of wine. I poured myself a schnapps, grabbed the afghan and pillow from the living room sofa, and shuffled down the hall to my office.

I was inching away from my marital bed. First I had simply turned my back (she turned hers first), then I landed on the living room sofa, and now I was headed for my office, where I could close the door and lock it from the inside. Soon I'd be on the front steps, hailing a taxi. The thought terrified me. I loved and needed Ruthie even as she pushed me away. She and the baby were the only family I had. I had even grown fond of Meyer and Mama Lenski—parents-in-law are better than no parents at all.

My marriage was not ending in sudden death, but was wearing away like a soft fungus along the perimeter of a river, algaeous black water beating against its edges. A disease—call it apathy, call it laziness—had crept into our hearts and lodged there. The events of that night were merely a scraping away of the niceties, the way a restorer scrapes away layers of paint to expose the vibrant original surface beneath layers of dust and dirt.

Our infant son, the one bond that connected us, had nearly been decapitated by the blade of a sled, and in that moment when Ruth and I both envisioned his bleeding head rolling like a candy apple down the slope to the Hudson River, we each saw our futures—in that single instant—as severed and independent.

I closed and locked my office door, set my glass of schnapps on the rug, and lay on the couch with the afghan wrapped around me. I reviewed my schedule for the following day: four hours of patients in the morning, a lunchtime symposium at the Institute, analytic supervision in the late afternoon, followed by a new referral. At 8 P.M., Ruthie and I were to dine with her parents at La Grenouille. Not a bad day, in all. A day which would speed by on the wings of sheer momentum, like every other day preceding it.

I heard a sharp knock on the door.

"Solomon?"

I didn't answer right away. My heart pounded. My wife was a wee scrap of a thing, but I was afraid of her.

"Solomon, I know you're in there!"

I reluctantly went to the door and opened it. She stood there, enveloped in an old silk kimono, her arms folded across her chest.

"What are you doing in here?" she asked.

"Finding yet another place to sleep," I responded.

Pain flickered across her face, wrinkled her smooth brow. I knew I could reach out to her, that I could pull her toward me and stroke her cheek; instead, I remained rooted in place, hands heavy by my sides. The moment passed. Ruth was a lovely woman. If she had not been my wife, if she had been an utter stranger walking down the street, I would have wanted her. I would have gazed at her tiny waist, her cleavage, her tapered ankles—but now I barely noticed her that way. She was the mother of my child, sharer of my chores, the back turned away from me in the night.

"Solomon, I was frightened," she whispered. "I thought—"

"I know what you thought," I said bitterly. "You thought I had put Daniel in danger."

"It's just he's all I have."

She began to cry.

"You have me, Ruthie," I say.

"No—I—don't—"

Her breath was coming in big gulps. Her nose was running, but she made no attempt to wipe it. Huge tears ran down her face, dripped off her chin.

This is the tyranny of marriage: the vows which bind us allow us to become our worst selves. Thrown dishes, slammed doors, faces contorted like an infant's—all part of the contract. No one tells us this. No one tells us that the only unconditional love in this world is between parent and child. I have loved Daniel for thirty years, even though I haven't known him. I have stared at his picture each morning, and called to him in my dreams. But passion between a man and a woman is finite. If it lasts a thousand days, count yourself among the lucky.

I pulled her to me. The top of her kimono was damp, and she smelled vaguely of formula. Her breasts flattened against me, her mouth soft against my neck, and as we stood still for a few minutes, feeling each other's hearts slow, I found myself stirred by her.

"It's just we tried so hard to have him—all those doctors, the tests—I just couldn't bear it if—"

"I know, sweetheart. I know," I murmured.

She looked up at me as I brushed a wet strand of hair from her cheek. Her eyes were small and red.

"Come to bed, Sol. Please."

I followed Ruthie into our bedroom, where I had not slept in over a month. We walked upstairs, past the gallery of photographs, our ancestors blended together, Auschwitz and Park Avenue touching hands. I stood by the foot of the bed and watched as she laid herself out for me like an offering. She opened her robe, stretched out her perfectly smooth legs and waited, flushed, expectant.

"Come here, Solomon."

I crawled next to her. She was all pale creamy flesh and old silk, and I was still fully clothed. She undid my pants, bent over me and untied my shoes, yanked off my socks. It all fell in a tangle to the floor. Her breasts, pendulous since Daniel's birth, swayed above me and I focused on the gentle curve of her stomach, down to the soft curl of the hair between her legs. The afghan fell away from my chest and she pushed it off the bed with an exasperated sigh. "So many clothes," she mumbled. Her hands were ravenous. Did she know it would be the last time we would ever touch each other? That our thousand days had long since expired?

I ran my hands over her curves, but I could not feel her skin. There was an invisible barrier between us, a wall which rose up between our two naked bodies and stopped desire in its tracks. Could she feel it too? Her skin was pink, glowing. She reached for me desperately, fingers skimming over my collarbone, my ribs, and down my belly. I closed my eyes. Was she in for a disappointment! Her fingers wrapped around my limpness and she inhaled sharply.

I tried to concentrate, but I became even softer from the effort: any fantasy that did not include Ruthie only deepened my guilt. I even tried to summon the Ruthie of my courtship, the premarriage Ruthie whose soft, enveloping flesh never failed to entice me. I conjured up our first kiss, her tentative tongue, the first time I reached beneath her cashmere sweater, unhooked her bra, and cupped one warm breast in the palm of my hand.

It wasn't working.

"Ruthie." I gently removed her hand and held it. "Sorry, sweetheart."

She rested her head on my shoulder.

"God, Solomon—"

"Equipment failure," I grinned feebly. "Maybe it was the schnapps."

She began weeping. I reached down and groped for the blanket on the floor, scooped it up and wrapped it around both of us. I searched her wide brown eyes for something familiar—something to pull me in.

"What's happened to us?" she moaned.

"I don't know, dear," I answered quietly, kissing her temple.

"I never thought marriage would be like this—"

"Like what?"

"Lonelier than alone."

Daniel began wailing in the nursery, but neither of us moved. My house was a symphony of high-pitched sadness that night, and all I could do was listen. I stroked Ruthie's brow: She was perspiring, her armpits pungent. Had I once liked this scent? I despised myself as I leaned down to kiss each salty eyelid. I loathed the invisible wall which had been built when neither of us were looking.

I hoisted myself up and sat on the edge of the bed. This is a posture assumed by men everywhere: back bowed, head in hand, knees slightly parted. You will find men in adobes, tenements, and mansions seated on the edges of their connubial beds, backs turned like blistering fruit against the sun.

"You started all this," I lashed out.

"What do you mean—?"

"All the tests, the doctors, the drugs—you couldn't just let nature take its course."

"I wanted a child!"

"After jerking off into test tubes for two years, it's not so hard to understand why I can't—"

"Solomon!"

"I'm just calling it like it is, Ruth. Making love is not sitting in a doctor's office looking at *Playboy*—"

"But we used to joke about it!"

"Well, it's not so funny now," I said bitterly.

34   I couldn't even look at her as I hurled these insults. Instead, I focused on the mustard-colored fringe of our bedroom rug, a piece of which was stuck beneath the heavy walnut bureau—I would have to fix that sometime soon. I heard a faint buzzing in my ears, a noise which told me I was going too far, that the delicate wire which snaps a marriage in two was about to be crossed.

"You almost killed him today."

She said it quietly, with no inflection. *You almost killed him today. Please pass the salt.*

"Ruthie, he was never in any danger. You've totally blown this out of proportion."

"You almost killed him," she repeated shrilly, as if the power of her own words somehow made it truer.

The buzzing in my ears grew louder.

"That's it. I've heard enough."

I uttered the ancient words of retreat between husband and wife, so old they must be biblical. Adam might have said this to Eve. Abraham to Sarah. They felt like flat champagne in my mouth. I stood, stretched my arms over my head, then grabbed my robe and a magazine from the bureau and walked to the bedroom door, hovering there for a moment.

"I'm sorry, Ruthie," I said gruffly.

She had turned her back and was now curled into a little ball, facing the window overlooking Riverside Park. A car drove past our house, headlights sweeping through the darkened room.

"It's not you—it's me. I have to sort myself out," I said in one last attempt to leap over the gulf between us.

She curled tighter into the fetal position and wept so violently her body shook beneath the blanket.

I walked to the side of the bed, bent down to kiss her forehead, and she pushed me away so hard I staggered. *At least I tried*, I thought to myself as I closed the bedroom door firmly behind me. *I'm not such a sonofabitch after all.* I thought I had exhibited great dignity. I did not slam. I did not yell, or scream, or cry. I blocked my ears against the sounds of my wife and child, and padded back downstairs to my office.

As I lay on my couch and closed my eyes, the magazine folded over my chest, I knew Ruthie was right on two scores: I had almost killed my son. And there was no loneliness like marriage.

Three

Even before you were born, I knew you would be a survivor. You clung to your mother's womb like a soldier in a trench. Five times during Ruthie's pregnancy she began to bleed, and each time the miscarriage stopped miraculously, confounding the doctors. You were a rock climber, sky diver, secret agent. "Hi, this is Dan." I can hear it in your voice: the sharp edge I have kept inside me all my life, twisting and puncturing any chance of my own happiness—you have that same edge. You wield it like a weapon. You carry it like a blade.

Travel brings out my need for order. My bags are lined up near the front door—old luggage, but elegant, in the best of taste—another relic Ruthie left behind. I have briefed my secretary, and left a list of covering doctors. They have all been carefully chosen. They are young enough to have missed the headlines of thirty years ago, and they are not members of the Institute where my name still invokes a collective shudder. If they have heard anything about Solomon Grossman, it has been no more than a murmur. New York, it turns out, is a pretty big town. Even in the incestuous world of psychoanalysts, there are many different circles.

My taxi driver today is from a country that no longer exists. His name has no vowels. His radio crackles with the music of his defunct nation, and his car smells of air freshener and tinfoil wrapped falafel, humus spilling over the edges.

"JFK," I tell him, after hoisting my bags into the trunk myself.

He turns and looks at me blankly.

"Airport."

"Ah, airport, La-gar-dee," he grins.

"No. *Kennedy.*"

"Kennedy." He places an index finger against his temple and pulls an imaginary trigger. Laughs. I glance at his name again, then at the talismans hanging from the rearview mirror, and realize all I have to do is invoke the name *Salman Rushdie* and I'll be good as dead myself. In other circumstances I would get out of his cab, but today there is no time. Cabs are scarce on Riverside Drive, and I want to make my flight, not create a ripple of political enlightenment. Who knows—a number of cabdrivers have already been implicated in the recent bombing of the World Trade Center—perhaps I have walked into an international terrorist conspiracy. Perhaps this driver is not taking me to the airport at all, but to a small, delapidated building in Queens where I will be bound, gagged, and held hostage. What would they want with me? And is there anyone in the world to pay my ransom?

Someone has left a *New York Post* on the backseat—this morning's edition, with a photograph of the L.A. crash on the front page. The cockpit of the plane lies on its side, smoke still steaming from its edges. The wreck seems alive, as if a giant creature might emerge at any moment and shake itself free. THE DEADLY SKIES, reads the headline. Inside, there are more graphic photos. Bodies covered with blankets, limbs bent at impossible angles.

"You take plane?" the driver asks.

"Yes."

"Neeeeerrpphh," he wails, simulating, I suppose, the sound of a plane crashing.

"Thank you," I say.

The FDR Drive is jammed, so he makes a screeching turn onto Third Avenue and heads uptown. Just as well. We weave through Spanish Harlem toward the Triboro Bridge. I prefer this route myself. More colorful than the highway. We pass bodegas and tenements, stolen electronic goods being hawked on the sidewalk next to spanking white Camaros, boom boxes blaring. This used to be Katrina's territory. I can almost picture her crouched on the street, camera aimed at the door of a crack house, waiting for disaster. I close my eyes for a moment. Inhale deeply. What are the first senses that disappear when memory fades? When someone we love disappears —what do we forget first? The way they looked? Smelled? Tasted? Felt?

When I try to breathe in Daniel, all that's left of him is the sweet, powdery scent of infancy. I used to bury my nose in the top of his head and inhale as if I could somehow ingest his essence—as if I knew I would have to hold my breath for the next thirty years. Now he is a grown man, and that scent is long gone. The Daniel Gross of this morning's news probably smells of aftershave, tobacco, sweat, the vague, fishy scent of a woman lingering on his fingertips. Ah, listen to me. I am assuming a great deal. I step outside my office and it is as if I have never heard the word "projection." He may be a health fanatic who subsists on the juices of green plants. He may have converted to Buddhism, taken a vow of celibacy. What do I know? Thirty years is a lifetime. Daniel's *whole* lifetime, in fact. He has gone from a cawing infant with the pure scent of a newborn pup to a government official with enough frequent flier miles to go to the moon.

I feel like I'm flying into a black hole. I thought life had knocked all the spontaneity out of me—my last reckless impulse cost me my family and reputation—but this morning, I improvised! I dialed the airline and reserved one first-class seat to Los Angeles (moments of grand gesture should be grand all the way—champagne! caviar! terry-cloth booties!) and I was utterly calm. Solomon, I told myself, this is your life—right here, right now.

I avoid at all costs the very real possibility that my son will hate my guts. I will do anything to stave off the menacing thoughts crowding my head: that he will spit in my face, call me names, refuse to see me. Perhaps he has become an Orthodox Jew and has already sat shiva for me, rending his clothes, saying the mourner's kaddish, killing me off in his heart. Maybe his mother told him I was dead, or worse— never told him about me at all. *Your father was a navy commander drowned at sea,* she might have whispered. Or: *your father was a wartime correspondent held hostage on the Gaza Strip,* as she smoothed his hair away from his shiny brow so like my own. *Your father? You never had one. You were created in a petri dish at America's first experimental sperm bank.*

THEY HAVE DELAYED THE PLANE at the gate for an hour. Mechanical trouble, they say. There is grumbling all around, a collective murmur, but I don't care. What's an hour, after a lifetime? Besides, in first class, they reward us for this delay: fresh-squeezed orange juice and champagne flow freely; my glass is constantly replenished by a stewardess who leans forward in a cloud of Shalimar. I can't imagine what it's like for the poor people squeezed into economy class with all their screaming babies. If God had wanted us to fly he would have given us wings—just check out the scene at LAX—but babies are particularly unable to bear the sensation of a plane lifting into the air. Their little eardrums go pop, pop, pop, as if somewhere in their tiny brains they sense that twelve thousand tons of metal cannot logically rumble into the air. As we grow older, we become inured to this fact. We simply do it. We risk our lives every day in innumerable ways—so that getting on an airplane seems safe in comparison.

I have never before flown first class, not even when Ruthie and I were together. The Lenskis didn't believe in wasting money, though they certainly liked to spend it. A comfier seat and bad champagne were not worth the extra penny to my beloved ex-in-laws. Five hours is five hours, I can almost hear Meyer kvetching. The money won't get you there faster. This is how the rich get richer. They thought nothing of buying their precious daughter a brownstone, but the oriental in their own living room was threadbare.

The poor child next to me, an elegant girl in her late twenties, is quaking. Her hand trembles as she raises a glass of champagne and orange juice to her lips. A self-help book lies open in her lap. I am tempted to comfort her, but I don't want to begin a five-hour analysis. Is she trembling because of our "mechanical difficulties"? Because of yesterday's crash? Flying should be the least of her concerns. We will soon be on our way, the shiny 747 hurtling safely through the air to its destination, the City of Angels. After all, this is what airlines do, day after day, hour by hour, one flight after another. The odds are utterly stacked against two major plane crashes in twenty-four hours. The airlines are fond of citing such statistics: it is safer to fly than to drive a car, ride a motorcycle, cross the street.

I'm sure the passengers of World Air 103 took great comfort in these statistics as they snapped their seatbelts firmly into place and flipped determinedly through in-flight magazines, ignoring the stewardess's pantomime-with-oxygen-mask in front of the cabin. By the time World Air 103 exploded, the bright orange masks probably hadn't even had time to drop from their aerodynamically designed hiding places.

I lean over to my panicked traveling companion.

"Feel free to talk to me," I say in spite of myself, "if you think it will help."

She looks up from her self-help book and takes me in.

What does she see? Sometimes I walk down Broadway and catch a glimpse of myself in the mirrored panels of store windows. Who is that old man? I wonder in the moment before I realize it is me.

The girl shakes her head and returns to her book. *Return to Love.* How far, in her short life, can she have strayed from love in order to necessitate a return? I examine her out of the corner of my eye. Everything about her is frighteningly perfect: her legs are well toned, clean-shaven. Her nails are red ovals. Her hair has been carefully set, then combed out to look artfully tousled. She is not beautiful, but has that healthy Nebraskan farm girl look that Procter & Gamble has decreed equally appealing to men and women. After all, women are the ones who actually buy the toothpaste, aspirin, soft drinks this girl probably hawks on national television. She must have to fly all the time. Does she have parents? Do they take care of her?

She suddenly slaps the book closed. "Every flight has high crash potential and low crash potential," she says evenly, staring straight ahead. So it is flying nerves after all, I think, proud of my deductive powers. I will play along.

"Sorry?"

"This flight has high crash potential," she repeats.

"How's that?"

"These people"—she waves her hand at the heads poking above blue upholstered seat cushions—"look like victims."

She leans toward me intimately.

"I always scan the waiting area before I get on a plane. If they look like a bunch of losers, I take the next flight."

"And today?"

"Today I had no choice. I have to be in L.A. tonight."

"And you?" I ask. I cannot resist the Socratic urge. "Does this mean you're a loser?"

She smiles wanly. "Let's just say I don't think God would keep the plane up in the air just for me."

"Ah, but I will give you two reasons why you're safe on this flight," I tell her. The champagne has gone to my head. I feel a slight swaying, even though we have not left the gate. I am a dispenser of free advice and good will. Ladies and gentlemen, the doctor is in.

"Yes?" She looks at me with the world-weary expression of a child who has flown straight from the plains of Nebraska to the monoliths of Madison Avenue.

44   "First of all, this plane won't crash because there was a crash yesterday. These things don't happen one after the other. The odds are against it."

"What's the second reason?" she asks, unconvinced.

I lean forward and whisper in her ear.

"Because of low crash potential."

"And why is that?"

"Because I am on this flight," I declare grandly.

But she continues to look uncertain, my little chickadee.

"And who are you?"

I wave her away, feigning annoyance. I know she doesn't mean to be rude. She doesn't even realize she might be insulting me. Terror does this to people. What would I do if I believed I was about to die? I would pray. Not because I believe in the existence of God or of his specific interest in a white-haired, stooped-over shrink named Grossman, but out of some muddled theory of the collective unconscious, in the hope that my son would receive my prayer in his sleep and awake the next day stronger and more resilient without ever knowing why.

Prayer is simply the language of longing—not unlike psychoanalysis. Perhaps I should have been praying instead of analyzing these many years. After all, what will happen when I can shake Daniel's hand, grasp him in a bear hug? Will all the longing seep out of me in a slow, steady leak? I can see it now, bilious green, forming a puddle on the ground beneath me. What will I be without this longing? It has defined me for so many years I imagine it is the glue which keeps me together.

THE PLANE HAS PULLED AWAY from the gate. The girl next to me has closed her eyes, and her lips are moving. Is she praying? I doubt it. More likely she's repeating one of those odious affirmations so popular on the West Coast these days. I *am okay, I am okay, I am okay.* Desperate measures for desperate times. New Age Band-Aids for asthmatic souls.

Her fists are clenched.

I-am-okay-I-am-okay-I-am-okay.

The pilot announces that our mechanical difficulties are a thing of the past. As we lumber down the runway, she suddenly reaches over and grabs my hand. Doesn't look at me, doesn't say a word. As the plane gathers speed, I stare at her hand. Her palm is damp. Her fingers are long and tapered like a pianist's, and she is wearing two antique rings, one on her pinkie, the other on her ring finger. Both are platinum with small diamond and ruby chips, precious heirlooms passed down by a grandmother or maiden aunt.

Queens disappears beneath us.

"See?" I ask her. "We're safely off the ground now."

I realize this statement is an oxymoron. Her lips are still moving. *I-am-okay-I-am-okay-I-am-okay.*

THE STEWARDESS STOPS by with her omnipresent bottle of champagne. She leans over my meditating friend and replenishes my glass. I sip my champagne as we bump through the clouds, and feel a slight twinge in my chest. The small foil packets of salted almonds taste as good to me as the beluga caviar the Lenskis used to serve on New Year's Eve. For once this generic brand of airline champagne tastes better than all the bottles in Meyer's vintage cellar. Yes, it is the eve of a new year for Solomon Grossman, and the taste of victory is sweet in my mouth.

Five hours and thirteen minutes. I wonder if we'll be able to see the carnage from the air or whether all flight patterns will be diverted away from the crash site. *Ladies and gentlemen, those of you on the right side of the aircraft have a nice view up the coastline to Malibu. Those of you on the left side might want to lower your window shades now.*

On a movie screen in the front of the cabin, there is a tape of the national news from CNN. The crash has already been bumped down to a minor story. Tragedies have their fifteen minutes of fame, and then we move on. New bloodshed in Bosnia. Frank Sinatra has had a heart attack while singing "My Way." A patient who works for the *National Enquirer* has referred to this journalistic phenomenon as a "death watch." Journalists are flocking to the Florida hospital, waiting with pens poised for any news of Sinatra's condition. A turn for the worse makes a good story, but death makes an even better story.

Finally, the crash. A crater littered with fuselage. A wing slanted like a surfboard in the sand. The camera pans to an infant's bootie, thrown from a carry-on suitcase near a twisted piece of metal. Must they scrounge like vultures, picking through the rubble for the most heart-wrenching images? I pray my little friend doesn't look up from her mantra just now. If she sees this, no amount of mumbo-jumbo will help her. A glance at the other passengers confirms that I am not the only one fascinated by this juxtaposition. *This could happen to you*, the newscaster seems to be saying beneath carefully rounded vowels.

From the studio back to the crash site. A reporter squints into the camera, her heavy wool jacket a clear sign that she has just arrived from the airport herself. This one is an Asian girl, not nearly as cute as this morning's redhead. She stands with her back to the frenzy, and I squint at the scurrying, purposeful crowd behind her, scanning frantically for my son. Three seconds this morning were not enough. *Interview Daniel Gross*, I silently beg her. *Mr. Gross of the NTSB. Mr. Safety in the Skies.*

But there is no chance. The families have already begun to arrive, huddled beneath helicopter blades, shivering with shock in the sultry California dusk. Abject grief—*live! In per-*

son! Daniel is somewhere behind those whirring blades. I can picture him, Styrofoam cup in hand—does he take his coffee black, no sugar?—as he supervises his men combing the rubble for the black box, which has still, according to the reporter, not been located.

The captain announces that we have reached an altitude where the use of electronic devices is once again permitted. First class suddenly transforms itself into a multimedia spectacle: I count four laptop computers, three little earphone radios, two video games—whatever happened to books?

I rummage through my briefcase and pull out an interesting tome by a young psychoanalyst who gave up his practice in order to write books vilifying the whole miserable profession. I can't say I disagree with him, entirely. What good does it do, after all, to drag the unconscious from its clammy hiding place? And who is doing the dragging, anyway?

There are telephones in first class. This is something new. I have always liked to know how things work: the showers at Auschwitz, for example—was there one lever for gas, another for water? Could the Nazis tell their right hands from their left? Did it depend on their mood, or was there a more methodical plan?

How does a phone call float through the air with no wire attached to it? I stare at the gadget—Airfone, it's called, a concept so radical it can't be spelled properly—and decide I must use it at once. But who to call? I arise gingerly, careful not to disturb my companion, now blissfully asleep.

I stick my American Express card in the slot and bring

the phone back to my seat. I am oddly light-headed. Champagne, altitude, salted almonds. It will be a while before dinner. I feel along the bottom of my briefcase for a packet of Saltines. I need to maintain my blood sugar level. I am an athlete in training, running the marathon of all time. Success! I find the cellophane wrapper filled with smushed crackers and wash them down with another sip of champagne. I am dizzy with desire. I want the plane to fly fast, faster.

Inside my datebook, I find the yellow Post-It with Daniel's scrawled number. For the first time ever, I am in possession of my son's home and office numbers—a privilege most parents take for granted. Sunday evening phone calls, weekend visits, holiday meals are all part of the fabric of other people's lives. But I have never sat at the head of a Passover seder table filled with squabbling grandchildren, and most likely never will. *Are you listening? Are you now or will you ever be a family man? Fill my table with your brats. My halls pine for the shrieks of children.*

"Excuse me, are you using the phone?"

A corpulent businessman looms over me, breaking my reverie.

"Sorry, yes—I'll only be a few minutes."

I dial the numbers, pressing slowly. I think I hear the ocean through the receiver, like holding a shell to my ear. The call goes through. Amazing. When I was born, airplanes barely existed. Now you can make a telephone call from miles in the air.

"Hello?"

A woman's voice.

Think fast, Grossman.

"Hello?" Slightly more impatient.

"Hello, is Daniel Gross there?" I croak.

"No, he's not."

She's not forthcoming with more information. She does not say *No he's not, he's in California investigating a plane crash.* Or *No he's not, he's six feet tall and has blue eyes.* Or *No he's not, but I am his wife and the mother of our three children, one of whom is named Solomon.*

"Would you like to leave a message?"

"Is this Mrs. Gross?"

She laughs slightly.

"Why do you ask? What are you selling?"

Say something. Anything.

"This is Menachem Schneerson," I say, pulling a name out of a hat, realizing too late that it is the name of the great Lubavitch Rebbe who inspired the mitzvah tanks which rumble through the streets of Manhattan—Hasidic boys wielding tefillin who ask each passerby *Are you Jewish? Are you Jewish?* in the same adolescent murmur as the drug dealers next to them: *Smoke? Need a smoke?*

"Can I help you, Mr. Schneerson?"

Hah! She didn't catch it. Must be a shiksa. I feel, quite literally, a *ping* in my head. A rubber-band synapse which once held some piece of my psyche together has snapped.

"Yes, if you please. I must speak immediately with Mr. Gross."

"I'm sorry. He's out of town."

"But that is not possible! When will he return?"

"I'm not sure."

"But that is not satisfactory! I must know!" I practically shout into the receiver.

"I'm sorry, I—"

She sounds flustered. The poor girl—it doesn't take much to bully a perfect stranger over the telephone.

"If you please, what is your name, missus?"

My voice has taken on an accent that baffles me even as I speak, part German, part Yiddish—the immigrant voice I worked so hard to erase has returned full force in the persona of Menachem Schneerson, God forgive me.

"Where are you calling from?" she asks suspiciously. "You sound far away."

"Far away!" I gleefully howl. "I'm calling you from heaven!"

I glance out the window. It's not so far from the truth. We are flying into the setting sun, the clouds beneath us are tinged orange against the pale blue sky.

"Now hurry up and answer me, missus. This is one helluva toll call, believe you me!"

"What on earth—"

"I just told you, I'm not on earth."

Static suddenly crackles over the line.

"What the hell is going on?" she snaps.

"The voice of God!" I crow.

"Bullshit! You're in a goddamn airplane—"

The game is over. I quickly press the hang-up button on the phone. Can they trace calls a mile into the air? How far has this new technology gone? An average citizen can attach a gadget to his telephone to flash the number of the person calling. Heavy breathers, beware, there is no anonymity left in this world. I used to call Katrina once or twice a year. She was not difficult to find. I would read an interview with her in a glossy magazine, in which her latest habitat would be described and photographed: *Katrina Volk takes her café au lait each afternoon near her loft in the Marais.* Quite the wanderer, my Katrina. I meant her no harm. I would simply dial the number, wait to hear her voice, then hang up the phone. Now technology has denied me this small pleasure.

So who was this woman answering my son's telephone? Maid, girlfriend, wife, roommate? His answering machine's outgoing message did not say *we'll* get back to you. It was decidedly, defiantly a single man's message, with hard edges: it said *stay away.*

I have become nearly psychic, over the years, from listening to people's disembodied voices float up from the couch. I hear their histories unfolding in the cadences of their speech. And I am rarely wrong. I can locate childhood trauma, detect physical illness, find keys to locked doors of repression.

The more I think about it, what I heard in that girl's voice was a certain degree of ownership. A wife? Or perhaps his girlfriend. At the very least she is shtupping him, no doubt about that. Why didn't she tell me whether or not she was Mrs. Gross? She had the entitled, whiny voice of privilege I know so well. What a mouth on her! Like father, like son. Perhaps poor Daniel has chosen from the cream of the crop: a beautiful, educated thoroughbred just like Mama.

. . .

I THINK OF your mother only when prompted, say, in a doctor's office, while filling out forms. Check one: single, married, divorced, widowed. There should be an "other" box. Other: forsaken.

The night Ruthie left with you, the house moaned with silence. Each floorboard creaked beneath my feet as I wandered from room to room, opening and closing doors as if perhaps, by some sleight of hand, she had left you behind. I tried to sleep—first in my marriage bed, then on my office couch. Imagine my surprise when I woke up in the morning, my back aching, curled up on a mat near a pile of stuffed animals in your nursery.

You will want to know how I searched for you. You will want to hear that I spent my life's fortune, that I left no stone unturned. I will tell you that I hired detectives, spent thousands on phone bills, followed school buses down the winding roads of Greenwich, Connecticut. What you will not want to know is this, Daniel: I always knew where you were. It was not lack of knowledge—or certainly not desire—but a shame which seeped into me over the years from the ground up. First, I was forbidden to see you but eventually the choice was mine.

I will tell you only what you want to hear.

There is no room between us for the truth.

"SIR, WAKE UP!"

"Wha—?"

"You were crying in your sleep," says the girl. "You must have been having a nightmare. You've been asleep for hours—you missed dinner."

"Where am I?" I ask, completely disoriented.

This girl with soft blond hair brushing her shoulders—is

she an angel? Ruthie, Katrina, Menachem Schneerson—the margin between past and present, real and make-believe, all of it is closing in on me, blurring into a gray haze.

Well, folks, we're passing over Salt Lake City now, and if you care to raise your window shades you'll see—

"You're on your way to Los Angeles," she says soothingly.

"Los Angeles . . ."

There is a pounding in my head, a sharp pain between my eyes. Terrifying. I lift my hands to my temples and push down, as if it will fly off my body, be sucked out the emergency doors, and land in the center of Salt Lake City. What will the Mormons do with the freeze-dried brain of a Jewish shrink?

54   "Excuse me," I mumble.

I unclasp my seatbelt and stumble down the aisle to the bathroom. I have heard there are hidden video cameras in airplane lavatories. Somewhere in Washington, deep within an FAA vault, thousands of miles of tape are coiled like a nest of snakes, the bathroom habits of long-distance travelers preserved for posterity. Supposedly no one sees these tapes—they exist for security reasons only. I doubt it. Somewhere within the government lurks an anal-retentive voyeur who steals the tapes and makes home videos.

The hidden cameras could be anywhere: in the socket of the fluorescent light, behind the mirror. I do not want my humiliation on tape. I lean against the sink, holding my head, massaging my temples with both hands. I remove my blazer, unbutton my shirt, and scrutinize myself in the mirror—my eyes are bloodshot, pupils dilated. Not so good. I try to remember everything I learned in graduate school about strokes, edema, palpitations, blood pressure. I press two fingers against my aorta and count my pulse. Something is definitely wrong. This is not just anxiety. I try to assess the state of my own health: divorced white male, sixty-four. Nonsmoker, light drinker. Lives alone, no pets. Family history: father, deceased (stroke), mother deceased (heart attack). All other relatives deceased (asphyxiation). The back of my neck and chest is flushed. I cannot make a fist with my left hand. The toes of my left foot are numb, and my calf and thigh are tingling. I open my mouth, and it curls strangely up on the right side while the left side stays still.

Finally, my true face has emerged. With every smile, I appear to be snarling.

My short-term memory fades in and out, like a spool of damaged film. Some images are sharp, while others have been ruined. I know I am flying to Los Angeles on my way to see my son, but I can't remember whether I had breakfast or canceled my patients.

I sit on the toilet and rest my head in my hands. The lavatory is aswirl, the mirror reflecting me a dozen times over, a whole football team of Solomon Grossmans. What will Daniel see? I try to look at myself dispassionately: despite all the years of neglect, I am still—how shall I say it?—a distinguished gentleman. Hah! A refugee gentleman with a fancy-shmancy degree whose blue cashmere blazer and shock of white hair hide a multitude of lies.

Breathe deeply, Grossman.

Perhaps this is just a panic attack. The tingling palms, the cold sweat, even the pounding headache—all could be symptoms of terror. My heart's desire is within my reach. No small wonder I should be panicking. Breath *in*-two-three-four, *out*-two-three-four. I watch myself in the mirror until my features blur and I look like Charlton Heston playing Moses in The *Ten Commandments*. I test out my smile once again—my mouth is still slightly crooked.

Gentle rapping on the bathroom door.

"Are you all right in there?" calls my traveling companion.

"Yes, yes," I answer. I button my shirt and tuck it back into my trousers—amazing how much strength I have in one arm solely because of handwriting and masturbation—then grab my blazer and open the door.

"Can I help?"

Can I help. The three words I have most frequently uttered in my professional life are now leveled at me by a girl young enough to be my granddaughter.

In my inside jacket pocket I carry a pen and small notepad. Once I return to my seat, I carefully try to print my name. My hands are shaking, my handwriting a blur. I forget that I have business cards in my wallet, the impressive *Solomon Grossman, Ph.D.*, engraved in script. I write my address in New York, my bank, the location of the key to my safe-deposit box, and—I can think of nothing else. My life has boiled down to a few jottings and digits.

I hand her the yellow Post-It and the torn piece of notepaper.

"Please, if anything should happen, call my son and tell him I was on my way to see him."

The words come out in a rush, a single breath. The

pounding in my head eases somewhat as she folds the scrap of paper into her wallet.

"Oh, you'll be fine," she soothes.

I dig the sharp metal spiral of the notepad into the soft flesh of my left palm. Nothing. No pain, no twinge. And yet I can still move my hand. It feels heavy, as if filled with sand, but still my body has not betrayed me—only my mind, playing tricks. I will propel myself off this plane, across the vast caverns of LAX, and to the Hertz rental counter, where a mid-sized luxury sedan is waiting for me. I have to move slowly, like a tough-shelled bug. I will buy a frozen yogurt and a cup of decaf. And I will drive with my right hand, my right foot, on the right side of the freeways of Los Angeles. Shall I go to the hotel first, to freshen up? No, I think I will go straight to the wreck. After thirty years, there is no time to waste.

FOUR

THE PREVIOUS EVENING'S BLIZZARD had left deep drifts of snow piled along the sidewalks the morning Katrina Volk was scheduled for her first appointment. The plows had been groaning and scraping through the night, but Riverside Drive was still slick as a skating rink. Through my venetian blinds I could see cars spinning in semicircles, one after the next, like toy trucks in the hands of a toddler. I didn't think she'd make it. I was surprised when a taxi skidded to a halt and a pair of ski-booted legs emerged. She was all bundled up in a parka, but her head was bare, hair whipping around her face in the heavy gusts.

When I opened my office door, I was struck by an almost irrepressible urge to close it quickly in her face. Why didn't I want to work with this patient? I didn't know. All I knew was that I didn't want to meet the lanky girl who stood on the stoop. I didn't want to begin an analytic relationship with her that could last a year, much less a decade. But we do not really choose our patients any more than they choose their illnesses, and so I fought off my resistance, chalked it up to exhaustion, to the terrible row with Ruthie the night before. All night I had tossed and turned on the plush velvet of my couch—a comfortable place to spend fifty minutes, not eight hours.

I ushered her into my office and watched to see where she would sit. This first move in the chess game of psychoanalysis is always an interesting one. Will the patient select the couch or one of the Eames chairs? And what about body language: arms and legs crossed? Slumped into a C-curve? Erect and rigid as a sergeant? There are no surprises here; in any event, I am never surprised. There are only a few choices, and usually I can predict the most likely as soon as a patient walks in the door. Once a perch has been chosen, they inevitably become rooted there like homing pigeons.

Katrina sat in the center of the floor and unraveled her muffler, folding it carefully in half, then in quarters. Her cheeks were flushed bright red.

She pulled off her boots.

"Do you mind?" she asked. "My feet are soaked."

"Please," I murmured.

She was wearing red-and-white-striped socks. I was struck by the incongruity—these cheerful Santa Claus socks on this utterly serious girl. She crossed her legs, sat Indian-style, and stared at me.

This was the place for my opening gambit. *So, how can I help? What seems to be the trouble?* But instead, I said nothing. I folded my hands into a tent beneath my chin and watched her.

"I don't know why I'm here," she said softly.

I cleared my throat.

"Yes?"

One corner of her mouth lifted slightly, and suddenly she was ten years older. Her face was like one of those shifting computer images which had yet to be invented. One moment she was a child, the next, her face would crumble into the contours of an old woman.

"I haven't slept in nearly a month."

"Why, do you think?"

"My work."

"What is your work?"

"Photography. I'm a photographer."

It suddenly came to me. The most recent *Life* magazine photo essay on the self-immolating Buddhist monks of Hue— there was some sort of big deal because the photographer was a woman. A lovely young woman, at that.

"Ah yes," I said. "Now I recognize your name."

"You know it?" She seemed surprised.

"Yes, from *Life*," I said dryly.

"Those photographs were nothing," she said bitterly. "They chose the safest images—"

"Safe, how?" I asked, remembering images of charred corpses, smoke still rising.

"I took one picture," she said, "a close-up of a monk in flames. He was still alive. His teeth were bared, like fangs, almost, but his eyes seemed serene. He was at peace. It was the most beautiful image of all, but *Life* wouldn't print that."

"Beautiful?" It seemed an odd choice of word.

"Yes. His choice to die was beautiful."

"And so you are haunted by this monk?"

She buried her head in her hands. Her fingers were long, adorned by a single, silver ring with a blue stone at its center. When she finally lifted her eyes to meet mine, they were shining.

"Not the monk, no."

"What, then?"

"I—I'm not sure," she said softly.

I fell silent once again. Her gaze darted toward me, then away. She looked all around my office, as if searching for some totem which would tell her if I was trustworthy. I followed her gaze through the room: the box of Kleenex on the small table next to the armchair was nearly empty, and the spidery hanging plant by the window, which had seemed comforting when I bought it, now appeared overgrown. The tissue at the head of the couch still held the shape of my previous patient's head—in my haste I had forgotten to change it. I could see her thinking, the wheels in her head spinning out of control.

"I don't think I can do this. I thought perhaps I could, but—"

She began pulling on her boots, yanking so hard I was afraid she would hurt herself.

"Wait!" I said loudly, startling myself. She was already twisting her scarf violently around her neck, throwing on her coat, stuffing her hands into her pockets, searching for gloves.

She stood in the center of my office, ready to bolt.

"Yes?"

Please don't go was what I wanted to say. I observed myself, as I had learned to do in graduate school, horrified.

"Let me at least try."

"I don't know—"

"Tomorrow," I said quickly. "Come tomorrow at three o'clock."

A corner of her mouth turned slightly up, in what I had already come to recognize as Katrina's pathetic version of a smile.

"Perhaps," she said.

And then she was gone.

THAT AFTERNOON I had two free hours before the Institute meeting. Attendance was all but required at the lecture series. The evening's topic was "Dreams and Countertransference," and Helena Deutsch was to deliver the keynote address.

I left a note for Ruthie on the kitchen table and headed for the library on Forty-second Street, the big one. Usually I made use of free hours by catching up on correspondence, making notes for lectures. But on this day I carried a sheaf of papers in my briefcase as I boarded the M4 bus, telling myself I was off to the library for a change of pace.

As the soaked, rattan seats of the bus extruded their moldy winter aroma, lumbering down Broadway, past the new Lincoln Center and the nondescript prewar apartment houses of midtown, past Times Square with its Marlboro Man blowing puffs of smoke into the air, I tried to push my new patient to the furthest recesses of my mind. A colleague in London had sent me an interesting paper on the use of psychotropic drugs in treating schizophrenia. I buried my nose in it, but images from *Life* kept diverting me: How could she snap away at a human life as it went up in smoke? What enabled her to be so unflinching in the face of a monk engulfed in flame? Why didn't she vomit? Faint? Turn her back? And why hadn't she slept in a month?

As I climbed the stone steps leading to the entrance, the library's lions seemed to roar at me. *We know why you're here, Grossman. You're not playing fair. Don't you think you should speak to your supervisor? When is your next session with your own analyst?*

I can actually remember my shoes making a soft *tap-tap-tap* against the marble floor that day, deliberate and rhythmic as a soldier on duty. I wondered if my reconnaissance mission was unethical. I knew it was a sign that I had gone off the deep end. But was it actually *wrong?* As I headed for the stacks, I pondered the abstract, theoretical answers to these questions. Why this patient and no other? I had always followed the rules, lived by the book. My notes were exact, my interpretations conservative. No patient could ever accuse me of inappropriate behavior. I was admired among my colleagues, though some may have found me slightly stiff. If I believed in erring at all—it was on the side of caution.

What would they have thought if they had seen Solomon Grossman slink through the stacks of the public library in the hour of a yellow-gray winter dusk, several books on modern photography tucked beneath his arm? Surely, they would have been shocked to see me pouring through each index, searching through the V's. Perhaps they might even have been suddenly ennobled by my moral demise! Self-righteous indignation is powerful fuel for psychoanalysts; given that we are not allowed to sit in judgment of our patients, nothing pleases us more than to sentence and convict each other.

My detective work was not an easy mission. Katrina was not yet in the same league as Lisette Model or Margaret Bourke-White and photography had not yet been thrust fully into the realm of art or even of commerce. But finally I found her. Here it was—hard data. Evidence. Something to hold in my hands.

Volk, Katrina. b. 1938 *(Berlin, Germany)—*

Born in Berlin, city of my own birth! My family fled in 1938. I was eight, she was an infant. I wonder, was she wheeled in her carriage past the courtyard of my school at the Rykestrasse? Did I shield my eyes against the sun and notice her mother, strolling through the streets of Berlin, tall and regal, puffed up with Teutonic privilege? We had yet to wear the yellow stars, but *our* passports had been stamped with crimson J's. *Jude*—the most frightening two syllables in the German language.

My parents and I left Berlin in early November; it was the week before what later became known as *Kristallnacht*. We were like barnacles on the side of a rusty boat, hanging on, bound to a Germany that long since had stopped having a place for us. My father was a violinist who continued to work through the *Kulturbund*, the cultural union that employed Jewish artists during the 1930s. He thought Bach string quartets could save him, I suppose. He believed music was universal, that it could heal across ideological and what we then called "racial" lines. Then he watched an oboeist and two cellists being marched off to a concentration camp, forced to carry a large Jewish star emblazoned with the words "God shall not forsake us."

We were the lucky ones. We were granted passports because the wind was blowing in the right direction that day, or the SS emigration officer had enjoyed his eggs for breakfast or felt a stirring for my doe-eyed Mama. My father always believed someone in the States had intervened on his behalf, had mounted a campaign to free the great German violinist Otto Grossman. But the truth, as I see it now, is this: my father was a middle-distance runner, a work horse of a violinist, an excellent sight-reader. A member of the *Jüdische Kulturbund* orchestra in Berlin, he became a third-string violinist in the Philharmonic a few years after arriving on these shores. It was not greatness that saved us. It was quite simply an act of the same capricious God who had forsaken the oboeist and two cellists. God, who slumbered as a fire swept through the house he had built.

Volk, Katrina, photojournalist, Life; b. 3 October 1938. Daughter of Hermann Muensch (deceased) and Greta Muensch (née Wachs). Stepdaughter of Kurt Volk. Dalton School (1955). Barnard College (B.A., Phi Beta Kappa, 1959). Art Students League.

I SEARCHED THROUGH all the current reference books available that might include a more comprehensive biography of Katrina, maybe supply more data on her family, but none existed. My heart was pounding as I hunched over the heavy texts, for all the world looking like a dignified scholar. What was I doing? No one knew better than I that the analytic dialogue was a process of discovery, an unfolding of history which I had just completely curtailed. What lunacy made me think I had to know the facts of Katrina Volk? And what could I possibly make of the way our lives had overlapped, at least peripherally? We were born in the same city, halfway across the world. She went to the same private school as my wife—in fact, they may have been there at the same time. Perhaps they had known each other! The thought filled me with a dread I couldn't explain.

She had first been published at age nineteen. Five years later, she was already included in Who's Who.

I looked up my own name in the weighty blue tome. *Grossman, Samuel. Grossman, Sylvester.* I was not listed.

THAT EVENING'S LECTURE on "Dreams and Countertransference" took its toll on me. Helena Deutsch spoke of desire in the analytic process: not sexual desire on the analyst's part, but desire to heal the patient as manifested in the analyst's dreams. Good suggestible soul that I was, I came home that night, put my head on the pillow, fell asleep, and proceeded to dream about Katrina. My dream was filled with the cratered streets of Berlin, 1938. I saw Katrina, not as an infant but as a young woman, gripping the sides of a barbed-wire fence so tightly her palms dripped blood. Katrina's side of the fence was lush with greenery. Tropical heat made her bare arms glisten with sweat, and her hair curled wildly down her back. Her dress was damp in front. On the other side, my family paraded by, wearing black-and-white-striped pajamas and caps, bare feet cracked and bleeding in the snow. An SS officer appeared at Katrina's side, kissed her tenderly on the forehead as he pulled his pistol from its holster, and, without glancing up, shot them all cleanly—my uncle, aunt, three cousins—a single bullet in each brain. Katrina leaned her head against the SS officer's shoulder. He grabbed her hands in both of his, and when he let go, the bleeding had stopped.

At a few minutes before three the following afternoon, Katrina rang my buzzer. By then, I had succeeded in pushing her out of my mind, focusing instead on my other patients. I did not expect her to show. I gently brought to an end my two o'clock, who gathered his belongings and let himself out of my office while I remained seated, as was my custom. But the moment the door closed behind him, I leapt to my feet and began pacing the outer edge of the oriental. I realized, as I tried to slow my breathing, that I had been praying all day that Katrina wouldn't show up. I glanced at the framed correspondence between Freud and Ferenczi—surely *they* would have understood this. These were *their* conflicts, and now they were mine. I debated with myself: Should I tell her that my schedule had changed, that I would be unable to treat her? Refer her to another analyst?

I fought off the voices and opened my office door. She was sitting cross-legged on the floor, back straight as a knife, eyes closed. Had my two o'clock stepped around her on his way out?

I cleared my throat.

"Miss Volk?"

She did not move.

I wanted to crouch down and circle her like an animal marking its territory. If I could have been assured that her eyes would remain closed, I would have observed her more closely, but I was afraid she would blink open and I would be caught in the act. But wasn't it my job to observe? What act did I fear?

Katrina's hair was pulled into a curly knot at the nape of her neck. She was wearing a black turtleneck sweater which zipped up the back; the top of the zipper was sticking up, almost touching the knot of hair. A half-torn label (Best & Co.) peeked out. I could see the outline of her bra through the thin knit, the slight bulge of hooks at the center of her back. Her sweater had pulled slightly from the waistband of her skirt and the sliver of skin that poked through looked like a pale peach belt. Again, she had removed her boots, but this time her feet were stockinged, surprisingly small and delicate.

A voice screamed in my head: *Get out of it, Grossman! Refer her to Watkins, or Garvey, or anyone else at the Institute. It doesn't matter. Just get her the hell out of here.*

"Miss Volk?" I repeated.

This time she opened her eyes.

"Come in. Please."

I preceded her into my inner sanctum. She looked around the room at the chairs, the couch, then lowered herself to the floor, graceful as Danilova. She gazed at me unblinkingly, like a small animal who comes across another of its species, quite suddenly, in a thicket.

Usually, silence did not bother me. I allowed it to descend over the analytic hour like a blanket. Even if patients fell asleep on the couch—and yes, it sometimes happened—I would not wake them until their time was up. Weren't they paying for this hour, silent, sleeping, or awake, fully conscious or utterly in the throes of delusion? I believed in this silence. It was part of the very fabric of psychoanalysis—yet now I felt it choking me.

Why are you sitting on the floor? Why such intensity? Why are you here? Of course, I said nothing. I continued to meet her gaze and wondered what was really going on beneath that lovely exterior—the insomnia was a symptom, but of what? Most of all, why had I been prompted to find out more about her?

Abruptly, she reached for her portfolio and began rummaging frantically through a series of black-and-white photographs. Her fingers riffling through the wavy white edges of the paper looked delicate and strong. I could picture her thumb and index finger focusing a lens, hand shielding the sun, heavy camera case slung over her shoulder.

"Here they are," she murmured, pulling three photographs from the batch, then handing them to me, face down.

Shmuck that I am, I couldn't help but feel privileged, though I knew her work was not why she was seeking my help. If anything, it was what kept her sane and alive. I thought of those images of destruction I had seen in the library. This patient needed to stare down the darkness like a child playing chicken in the street. Whatever wreckage she captured with her camera soon became her own. Only in the blackness of her darkroom could she control the images—expose them, frame them, change them any way she wished. If she chose, she could even destroy them.

I reached for the photographs.

"Self-portraits," she said.

I turned them over.

Impassivity is the hallmark of a good analyst. Composure under all circumstances is essential to the process. We are blank slates upon which patients draw their hostilities and desires. Sharp breaths, pursed lips, furrowed brows—all evidence of opinion or emotion is potentially damaging to the patient.

The top photograph looked like a landscape. A smooth, desert scene. A long slope with a shallow groove down the center, leading to two small hills at the very top. It took a millisecond for the words *self-portrait* to sink in. I realized it was Katrina's stomach I was staring at, her rib cage, belly button, the bottom of her breasts.

The quality of the print was extraordinary. She seemed to have been influenced by Irving Penn—it was evident in the platinum tone of the print, the stark delineation between her flesh and the velvet black background. There was no ruin in this photograph, no ugliness, not even a blemish on her skin.

I flipped to the next image: the round, twin shapes of two buttocks lifted high in the air. Beneath them, I could make out a slight tuft of hair, lighter than the backdrop, and again the sense was of a landscape. Two smooth igloos, perhaps, or glacial mountains to be climbed. I was conscious of her eyes on me. What was her purpose in showing me these photographs?

The last was a frontal assault. The most artful of the three, a direct shot of two breasts, nipples staring directly at the camera like the blank eyes of a lover. The aureoles were puffy like a little girl's, but the nipples were hard, as if excited by the prospect of being photographed.

I raised my eyes from photograph to patient. She was looking toward the window, at the closed blinds, as if she could see beyond them to the street below. There was a wistfulness to her gaze. *I'm on one side of a thick glass lens. I'm here, and you're all out there, and that's the way it will always be.* Or so she seemed—or I wished her—to be thinking.

I rested the photographs carefully against the side of her portfolio. These were not images that Katrina Volk's fans would ever see. These were the counterpoint, the antithesis of her subject matter. Her body was perfection, her limbs smooth and unblemished, a thin shell surrounding a bloody yolk. And she was not far from cracking. Was this her purpose in showing me the photographs? *I am not the wreck. The wreck is me.*

I sat back and waited. Slowly, her head turned from the closed slats of the venetian blinds. Her gaze was cross-eyed, unfocused. She smiled and pulled a strand of dark hair from the corner of her mouth.

"So now you've seen me," she said.

I was silent.

"Don't tell anyone."

I kept my gaze steady. I had to fight the urge to reassure her. *Don't worry. You're safe with me,* I wanted to say. But if truth be told I wasn't sure how safe she was.

"I slept through the night last night for the first time in a month," she said.

Katrina's whole posture softened, and for a moment I

saw that the toughness was an act, a false self—a way of hiding her peculiar innocence.

I glanced at the clock. It was nearly a quarter to four. My next patient would be ringing any moment. Where had the time gone? How long had I stared at the three photographs?

"We're nearly there," I said, my voice hoarse. "Do you want to make an appointment for another consultation?"

"No."

My heart skidded.

"I want to be your patient."

"Well, then."

Later, I would think about the euphoria. I would examine it like a doctor holding an x-ray to blinding fluorescent light, then summarily dismiss it.

"My fee is twenty-five dollars a session. I generally see patients in analysis four times a week."

She nodded.

"I will insist on the couch."

"Sorry?"

"From now on, when you come in, please lie on the couch."

She nodded again, almost meekly.

"I take the month of August off, and the two weeks after Christmas."

I leafed through my appointment book. I knew I didn't really have any extra hours, but I'd shuffle things around.

"Is this time all right? Three o'clock, Monday through Thursday?"

"Fine," she murmured as she gathered her things, returning the photographs to her portfolio, zipping it closed. I wondered what she'd do with her self-portraits. Did she have a special hiding place for them? Were there more? Did she burn them and watch her alabaster skin turn to ashes?

I walked her to the door. Before she turned the knob, I stretched out a hand. I thought there would be only one other time our hands would meet, at the termination of her analysis many years from now. Her palm was as cool and flat as the black-and-white images I had held only moments earlier. I saw a flicker behind her eyes, a thought skittering across the rocky terrain of her mind, but we had no time to pursue it. *What were you thinking?* I wanted to ask. *And how does my hand feel in yours?*

74

Months later, Katrina would tell me this: how she made a wrong turn leaving my office and walked, instead, down the long corridor leading to the kitchen. She passed our photography collection, the two Berenice Abbotts, the Edward Weston nude folded around herself like a raw stalk of corn, the Man Ray rayograph.

She walked lightly. The floorboards did not creak beneath her feet. A light was on in the kitchen and your mama was feeding you in your high chair. Ruthie's back was turned away from the door, cotton apron wrapped tightly around a brand-new silk dress as she spooned strained peaches into your eager mouth. She had the radio playing, a Bach cantata which she conducted for you with two wooden spatulas. You laughed and reached for your mother's soft, manicured hands, red nails glimmering like bright confetti.

You must have seen Katrina—your big blue eyes never missed a trick. What do you suppose she made of this domestic scene as she stood in the shadows of the hallway? Was her heart pounding? She knew she didn't belong there. Her eyes swept the room as methodically as the second hand of a clock, ticking all around. Finally she focused on the wall of family pictures: amid the Lenski country picnics, a black-and-white photograph of my Berlin relatives stood out in stark relief, a galaxy of yellow Stars of David stitched to their coats.

If only you had gurgled and reached out to her! If only Ruthie had sensed a pair of eyes on her back and whirled around to see the girl lurking in the doorway, our lives might have been so different. As it was, Katrina stood unnoticed, and gathered, with her prodigious powers of observation, enough evidence to convict and sentence herself —and me along with her—to hell.

FIVE

THE CITY OF ANGELS flashes smoggy gray as we bump
through the clouds, then dip slowly into our descent, sporadic
lights blinking across the vast tarmac of LAX like inverse
stars. It seems we are falling into the sky, that heaven is
beneath us. The wheels lower with a lugubrious rumble and
my traveling companion chants.

I strain to see the crash, but there is no sign of it. Perhaps they have already carted the carcass of World 103 to a
distant hangar, far from public scrutiny. Who, after all, can
look at a wreck and tear his eyes away? Entire traffic jams are
caused by the remains of accidents on the sides of highways.
There is a name for it—rubbernecking—which has always
sounded pornographic to me. And a plane crash—well, who
can blame us for craning our necks? For straining to see the
charred bodies lined along the edge of the runway in white
body bags like soft decaying teeth?

The girl holds my left hand, squeezing tight. For all I know she may be digging her nails deeply into my palm, leaving angry, crescent-shaped welts. I feel nothing. For the first time in decades, a magnificent creature is holding my hand, and God—who likes a good joke—has made me numb.

"Let's count," I say. "I'll bet we can't count down from twenty-five before we land."

Like kindergarteners, we chant in unison.

"Twenty-five, twenty-four, twenty-three, twenty-two—"

The colorful lights of airport hotel signs light up the night. Red Hilton, green Holiday Inn, red Hyatt, all blurring into a jumble, an electric, neon alphabet soup. Tiny blue lights line the runways. By the time we reach eighteen, the wheels touch the runway with a *ping*, the wind flaps rise like a bird's ruffled feathers, and by zero, we are at the gate.

MY FREUDIAN-TRAINED MIND never ceases to amaze me. As we disembark, making our way down a long, narrow tunnel (which, as it happens, is a deep shade of pink) connecting the jet to the bustling neon of LAX, I have images of birth trauma. Here I am, not even out of the tunnel and already I am damaged, thrust into a cheap, warm world of rent-a-cars, Burger Kings, and suntan oils.

My new pal is by my side, a large nylon knapsack emblazoned with a silver triangular *Prada* logo slung over her shoulder. (In my day, Ruthie wore Gucci or Vuitton. Now, status comes in the form of a nylon gym bag.)

"Is your son meeting you at baggage?" she chirps.

I am taken aback.

"My son—?"

"The note you gave me was for your son—" she falters.

"Ah. No, I don't think he'll be meeting me," I murmur.

I am having difficulty walking. Thank God for the little trolleys they have at airports nowadays. I push my small black bag in front of me. Function over elegance. I am an old man. People who notice us, if they bother, will think she's my granddaughter.

I do not tell her that I have no other bags than what I am carrying. I have come to the Golden Land like an immigrant, a supplicant supporting solely my own weight. We make our way slowly across the airport. Moving sidewalks— another marvelous invention. We stand still as we pass a Chrysler convertible in the middle of the airport, cordoned off by ropes; newsstands and novelty shops hawk tee-shirts and mugs for the Rams and Dodgers; a squadron of Korean businessmen swarm toward the airport exit, following a perky, orange-faced Californian tour guide. I feel like I'm in a parade.

A sharp pain stabs through my head, and I unwittingly gasp.

"Are you all right?"

I take a deep breath.

Please, not here, not now.

I look at her face, so smooth and young, and have a nearly overwhelming urge to lean across the moving sidewalk and rest my head against her breasts.

"Yes, fine." I try to keep my voice from shaking. "I'm not used to traveling—too much excitement."

My breath stabilizes again. She has become my good

luck charm, my angel, my one and only friend. Pity my time has come to say good-bye.

"I'm afraid I must leave you now," I say gravely as we reach the baggage claim area.

She stands on tiptoe and kisses me on the cheek.

"You make sure that son of yours takes care of you!"

I tip an imaginary hat to her.

"I will do just that, my dear."

She cocks her head and grins at me.

"Is he married?"

"My son?"

"Yeah."

She waits for my reply. How can I possibly tell her I don't know?

"I'm afraid he is," I answer.

"Oh well," she shrugs. "Win a few, lose a few."

I stand and watch as she trounces away, hair flying, knapsack bouncing—and wonder when I grew too old to be in the running. Her long coltish legs remind me of Katrina. I raise a hand to my face and feel the loose skin along the gray stubble of my jaw, the wrinkles beneath my eyes. The perks of old age have eluded me: I do not have grandchildren, a retirement dinner, a gold watch in honor of fifty years' service. Nothing to show for over six decades on the planet.

I am suddenly disoriented as my little friend disappears around the corner. It is business-as-usual as LAX travelers jostle past me, limo drivers carry signs. I wish I had thought to hire a limo. I'm too nervous to drive. It has been years since I've sat behind the wheel of a car. Everyone around me seems to have a purpose—rushing to an important date. I look around myself frantically, not sure where to begin.

I trudge past the rental car counter and head outside to a line of cabs. The warm air hits me and I immediately begin to perspire.

A tanned man in a Hawaiian print short-sleeved shirt intercepts me. He has the ruddy complexion and jowls of a heavy drinker.

"Need a taxi?"

"I'm not going far," I stammer, curious to see what's going to come out of my mouth. "Do you know where—they're taking—families of—"

"The World Air crash?" he interrupts with a sigh. "Oh, God. Oh, shit. Lemme take you over there, no charge."

He hoists my bag into the trunk and closes the door behind me, gallant as a chauffeur. As we wind around the ramps of LAX, he sneaks glances at me in the rearview mirror. I avoid his eyes, focusing instead on his hairy wrists, fleshy fingers against the steering wheel, the glint of his thick gold wedding ring.

He swings a left into the airport Hyatt.

"Here you go, sir. They're all inside."

I peel a five from my wallet, but he waves me away.

"Please. Forget about it."

I have learned, over the years, not to judge people by their outsides—Katrina, after all, had the face of an angel. Take this gentleman, for instance: he looks like a boozer, a card-carrying redneck. Yet here he is, bringing my bag to the curb, patting me once, his hand lingering on my back. Salt of the earth, we used to call them. In the Hyatt lobby, I catch a glimpse of myself in a gold-toned mirror: an eminent, white-haired scholar in a navy-blue cashmere jacket, an elder states-man visiting Southern California to give a keynote address. All I need is a monacle, or perhaps a cane; the charade would be complete.

My heart thuds as I see a sign posted on a large easel: NTSB *press briefing—Conference Room* 1. What if Daniel is here, just around the corner? Now that he is within my grasp, my hands are trembling. It is impossible to prepare for a mo-ment one has waited for a whole lifetime. I have imagined meeting Daniel in an outdoor café near the Ponte Vecchio, in the galleries of the Louvre, in the London Underground at Tottenham Court Road. I have supplied our imaginary meet-ings with silence and music (Pablo Casals playing a Brahms cello sonata) with birds and cigar smoke, a flock of pigeons set against a steel gray sky. This hotel lobby—an airport hotel, at that—I never pictured.

I stop at the front desk and ask if I can leave my suitcase with them. Unencumbered, I walk past the hotel bar where a group of young men are glued to a basketball game on televi-sion, then glide up the escalator to the conference rooms. How did I become a man with a mission? Such stealth. Perhaps I was a spy in another life.

I pad down the carpeted hallway, then peer through the diamond-shaped windows in the swinging doors of Confer-ence Room 1, unprepared for the pandemonium inside: at least a dozen television cameras are trained on a U-shaped table covered by heavy white linen, and at the head of the table there are three men wearing ties and identical navy-blue windbreakers, shifting uncomfortably in front of a bank of microphones and the cardboard emblem of the NTSB. Off to the side of this carefully composed tableau, a table is littered with paper coffee cups, half-eaten danish, ashtrays spilling over. I quickly scan the faces of the three men, as if I'm a contestant on a game show. *Will the real Daniel Gross please stand up?* The man on the left is dark-haired and jowly. The middle one is slight and sandy-haired, wearing glasses. And the one on the right is black.

My temples throb and my eyes sting as I push open the doors and try to look official as I walk to the far side of the room. I stand behind a television cameraman and pull out my small notepad and pen, although no one seems to be checking press credentials. After all, why would anyone want to crash this party? I search the table, the crowd pressing forward thrusting microphones, and am suddenly hit by a wave of fear: what if I'm mistaken? What if I somehow misunderstood this morning's newscaster—what if this whole thing has been a giant hallucination? My eyes dart into the corners. Where is he? Where's Daniel Gross of the NTSB?

"The cockpit voice recorder has been recovered and sent to Washington," says the jowly man.

Everyone begins shouting at once.

"When will you have more data?"

"What about the black box?"

"What was the captain's safety record?"

"What about the wing flaps? Aren't the wing flaps often the reason for—"

"One at a time, please! We'll be happy to provide more information as it becomes available," he responds. "Our men are at the site—"

At the site.

I shuffle out of the room and continue down the hall, past a few smaller conference rooms, past a humming ice machine, instincts sharpened like an animal lost in the woods. As I round a corner, I see a half-dozen bedraggled, dazed-looking men and women heading in my direction. They are being led by a man in a suit with a gray crew cut who wears a World Air pin attached to the lapel of his jacket. As they pass me, I hear the man say something about a World Air bus waiting downstairs to take them to the site. I spin around and become part of the group like a drop of water on the edge of a puddle, my own gray dazed state rendering me almost invisible.

I leave my suitcase at the Hyatt and climb into the minibus for the short ride back to LAX. I sit next to a young woman in a dark business suit who holds a crumpled tissue to her nose. Her eyes are red-rimmed, her cheeks blotched with grief. Her suit is wrinkled—she was probably wearing it when she got the news. Who did she lose? Mother, father, sister, husband? I want to reach over and pat her knee, wipe her cheeks with cool water, rub circles of comfort against her back. For over thirty years I have been deeply involved in the "talking cure," and what it has taught me is this: there is no substitute for the human touch.

"Who—did you—?" she gulps.

Oh, not this game again. Can't I live without lying?

I bow my head, shake it slowly, let it hang.

"Do you speak English?" she asks slowly.

I keep my head down, my own face flushed with shame. What business do I have here among the grieving? This bus is a funeral limousine—we are on our way to the mass graveyard at LAX—and I am an impostor in their midst.

The man across the aisle is muttering to a woman tightly holding his hand.

"They don't want us to see. They're afraid we'll sue. That's all they fucking care about. Lawsuits—"

"Sshh," she says softly. "Not now—that's not important now."

I look out the window, past my own reflection. The bus rumbles by a blur of airport hotels and gas stations, incongruous islands of palm trees curving across the night sky. My own face is superimposed on the landscape, a negative transparency, a smudged, two-dimensional ghost. In no time at all, we are back at the airport, winding our way up and around a network of ramps, gliding slowly past the land of the living: taxis drop passengers curbside, porters hoist baggage onto conveyer belts, tired women wait in station wagons, hazard lights blinking. We move beyond all that. Down a ramp, *authorized personnel only*, past a security guard who waves us through, and suddenly, improbably, into the netherworld of the vast runways behind LAX.

Strange, to be in a bus on an airport runway. To travel through a tunnel and, in an instant, go from being the largest vehicle on the road to the smallest. There are no jets anywhere near us, still there is the sense of being minuscule, engulfed. We rumble slowly over huge white runway num-

bers painted on the ground. The scale of life has changed—
this bus is the height of a 747's wheel—and soon we are a
small craft in the middle of an ocean, rocked by waves. Suddenly, terribly, seasick. We follow a path lit by small red
flares toward a dark horizon flooded with light. We are driving toward the scene of the wreck, but it seems the closer we
get, the less there is to see. A murmur all around. *Where is it? I
can't see anything. Hold on, isn't that—*

"The NTSB has already moved the fuselage to a hangar,"
says the World Air spokesman, now standing at the front of
the bus. "They've begun the process of reconstruction."

"Why?"

"I don't understand—"

"I thought we were going to the morgue—"

Everyone is speaking at once.

"If you'll all just be patient, there'll be a spokesperson
here from the NTSB," says the official as the driver pulls up
to a taped-off area.

I look again through the window as my fellow passengers rush for the door, a strange urgency propelling them.
Where's the fire? What do they think they will find on the
runway? The signs of disaster are almost prehistoric: the
tarmac is shattered, cracked as if an earthquake has split it in
two, and the crater is as wide as a riverbed, but empty and
charred, glistening with white stuff—probably the foam they
used last night to stop the blaze. Twisted shards of metal are
scattered across the concrete. There are men everywhere—not
a woman in sight—young men wearing dark blue slickers, the
huge white initials of the NTSB emblazoned across their
backs. Dozens of color-coded plastic sacks are guarded by two

men who sort through the rubble of suitcases, handbags, shoes with torn-off heels, a baby seat perfectly intact.

I hear a sound, a low moan, and realize it has come from my own lips.

"Sir?"

The World Air official is leaning over me.

"Need a hand?"

"Sorry," I murmur, allowing him to help me from my seat. I am an old man, after all. Even older than I look.

I follow him off the bus, then huddle with the small group of mourners near the crater spread across the runway, deep and inviting. A man in an NTSB slicker crouches down with a camera and shoots a pile of metal shards, glowing like white-hot embers beneath the fluorescent lights. I glance around and realize it is Katrina I'm half-expecting to see—this wreck would be right up her alley. I can almost picture her today, middle-aged but still regal, her long hair tucked beneath a baseball cap, her legs limber from a lifetime of crouching. She would now be fifty-five.

"Excuse me!" I hear a voice and whip around.

"Ladies and gentlemen, I know this is a difficult time for you all and we'll do our best to help you through it. My name is Daniel Gross, and I'm the safety officer in charge."

A slender man, his hair blown across his forehead by the wind, shouts over the loud hum of the generator. *Not my son* —the thought trounces through my head. *Not my son*—this grown man in an official navy-blue windbreaker, his face drawn and haggard in the floodlights. He scans the small crowd, his eyes skimming over me with the same professional disregard as he takes in the rest of the next-of-kin. He has shadows under his eyes—Ruthie always had dark circles in the morning. He thrusts his hands deep into the pockets of his windbreaker.

"I know you folks asked to see this, but at this moment, we don't really have much to show you," shouts this weary stranger. "But this is a talented, well-coordinated team of people from NTSB, the Los Angeles Police Department, LAX security—and let me reassure you, we *will* get to the bottom of what happened here."

There is an undercurrent beneath his words, a wiry, tightly coiled tension ready to explode at any moment—*please leave*, he seems to be insinuating, *and let us get on with our work.*

"Where's my daughter!" shouts a woman behind me. "Why can't I see my girl!"

Daniel rubs his eyes hard.

"Ma'am, all the victims have been taken to the—morgue —at Centinela Hospital."

She lets out a wail like a siren's call, and Daniel looks around helplessly, the contours of his face slackening in distress. *Get her out of here!* In the softening of his eyes I see a glimmer, the briefest hint of the child in the man. *My son.* The blood races through my veins. My fingertips tingle with insane joy. I want to break free of this grieving crowd and gallop toward him, a lunatic stranger, and clasp him into a bear hug as the debris of one hundred and thirty-eight lives swirls in the darkness around us.

THE FIRST TIME I SAW YOU after the divorce was at your grandfather's funeral. There were dozens of dark-suited people mill-

ing outside Riverside Chapel, and the side street was clogged with limos. Nowhere other than Grossinger's on Rosh Hashana could you imagine a more homogeneous gathering of affluent Jews. Specks of gold and diamonds glittered in the sunlight; belt buckles, heavy watches, thin necklaces roping around the crepey necks of dowagers. I kept my eyes glued to the ground, as if Meyer Lenski could reach up and grab me from the grave—or from the casket, as it were—and make good on his whispered threats of what would happen if I didn't stay away.

It was at that moment that I saw your mother, emerging from a limousine. I almost didn't recognize Ruthie, she had grown so angular. She was like a shadow of her former self—no, not a shadow at all —in fact, her thinness had sharpened her looks. Now she was pure bones in the sunlight. The line of her jaw was clean, and her cheekbones jutted beneath her dark sunglasses. She had grown up, my ex-wife. And how. I felt a minor surge of pride at having had anything to do with the elegant, worldly woman who walked slowly into the chapel, her head held high, a small black veil drifting from her hat like a storm cloud. Her lips were perfectly outlined in red, dramatic against her pale, powdered skin.

Then behind her, unfolding your gangly legs, there you were. There was no mistaking you. The Lenskis may have taken you away, but they could do nothing about the genetic imperative, the stubborn peasant genes marching through your system. The Grossman nose, the Grossman eyes, the Grossman cleft of chin—I can only imagine their dismay when they saw their grandson transforming slowly, over the years, into a physical replica of the man they hated most. Hah! God is good.

Ruthie did not look my way as she walked into the chapel. She strode like a goddess or a politician, glancing neither left nor right.

But you, who trailed behind her—you looked straight at me. My knees nearly buckled when our eyes met—was it possible? Would you recognize me? At least unconsciously, it must have been like looking into a mirror, distorted and cracked perhaps, ancient and covered with grime, but a mirror, nonetheless.

It would not be too self-serving to say you were beautiful—I knew your beauty was of the childhood sort, that you would grow up to be an interesting-looking, Semitic man who would be best described as distinguished. But back then, you were a lovely boy, if a bit wiry, on edge as your eyes darted around the crowd. Your energy seemed coiled inside you, ready to spring at any provocation.

But of course it was I who was projecting these thoughts onto you. I who was ready to spring into action. I wanted to leap over the crowd and snatch you in my arms, kidnap my own son. Instead, I stood still, feeling my insides shrivel against my own impotence, opening and closing my hands, gasping for air as I watched you march into the chapel behind your mother.

IT HAS BEGUN TO RAIN, a soft drizzle smudging the chalk marks along the edges of the wreck. The tarmac has a rich sheen in the darkness, a fluorescent spotlight glowing like a full moon reflected in a smooth, placid lake. The men in windbreakers have pulled up their hoods. They work quietly, almost stealthily, sifting through the ruins like archaeologists unearthing an ancient city.

I watch my son as he strides away from us, crossing to the other side of the taped-off perimeter, past security guards who look like they mean business. He flips up his hood, moves around the scorched silver engine lying on its side, and disappears. I begin to cough—a loud, hacking cough which doubles me over, and before I know what's hit me the cough has turned to sobs. Tears stream down my cheeks, and the people around me murmur kindly, pat me on the back, offer tissues. They hold on to my arms as we move together, like one shuddering creature, through the drizzle to the bus. I hold a tissue to my mouth and stifle my sobs as we pull away from the wreck.

As we drive through the tunnel connecting the runways to the outside world, I move down the aisle, clutching seat backs.

"I'd like to get off at the terminal," I bend down and whisper to the driver.

"Sir—how can I help? What is your name?" interrupts the World Air official.

"I'll get off at the terminal," I repeat more loudly. I hear the desperation in my own voice, the edge that makes his eyes dart away.

We are whizzing past all the airlines. TWA, American, World Air, Continental. A nod from the official and the driver slows to a stop.

"Please, I really think it would be better if—" he implores, but I am already yanking at the doors.

"Let me out," I say civilly.

The doors swing open, and, with an apologetic glance at my fellow passengers, I climb gingerly down the stairs and walk through the sliding doors of LAX. My heart pounds and my head buzzes with confusion as I stand in the center of the terminal, looking around. I am hit by a wave of sadness so intense it stops me in my tracks. Only a few hours have passed since I arrived in Los Angeles, and already I have seen my son. Why didn't I go up to Daniel, out there on the runway? I told myself it wasn't the appropriate time—and without a doubt, it was not. But what really stopped me was terror, pure and simple. Fear that he would push me away from him, spit on the ground near my feet. Fear that he would look at me quizzically and tell me I must be mistaken, that he has a father he's known and loved all his life.

I make my way to the rental car counter. My reservation is still in the computer system. I am handed paperwork for a blue Chrysler convertible with a soft white top, and board yet another bus, this time traveling in the opposite direction, to the rental car place a few miles from LAX.

IT HAS BEEN YEARS since I've been behind the wheel of a car, and decades since I've negotiated the streets of Los Angeles. I feel like I'm in a spaceship as I press my right foot to the accelerator and the car lurches forward. I hand the guard my rental agreement, then drive over sharp spikes, past a sign warning me that severe tire damage will result if I back up. Danger surges white-hot through my veins. I am driving a car down the boulevards of an unfamiliar city, my foot heavy against the gas pedal.

I pull to the side of the road and consult a map. The street signs—Sepulveda, Centinela—are all strange and foreign-sounding. I have only one destination. I find my way back to the airport Hyatt.

The concierge recognizes me.

"Ah, sir! Your bag!"

I had actually forgotten all about it.

"Thank you," I say distractedly as he hands me my small suitcase. "Actually, I have another request. Are the NTSB people staying here?"

"Ah—" His eyes flicker. Clearly he's not supposed to supply anyone with this information. And, even more clearly, they are.

"I'd like to leave a message for Mr. Gross," I insist.

"One moment, please."

As he scans his computer, I notice an impossibly green palm tree next to the reception desk, its waxy leaves veined symmetrically with thin white lines. I reach out and rub a single leaf between my fingers.

"That would be *Daniel* Gross?"

"Yes." My heart leaps.

He hands me a message pad, and I carefully print. Be steady my hand: Mr. Gross. *It is imperative I meet with you as soon as possible.*

I hesitate for a moment, pencil hovering.

"Excuse me, but if I wanted to have lunch with someone working at the airport, where would be a good place to meet?"

"The airport restaurant would probably be your best bet," says the concierge. "You can't miss it. Looks like a cross between a spaceship and a tarantula."

I will be sitting at the bar of the airport restaurant at noon tomorrow. I am an older man with white hair, wearing a navy-blue jacket. It is an urgent matter. Thank you.

SIX

"I DREAMT ABOUT MY FATHER last night." Katrina's voice
rose dreamily from the couch. The only sounds in the room
were of my pen scratching on a stenographic pad and the
incessant hum of the air-conditioner. I remember it was a hot
day near the end of July. Ruthie and Daniel had already gone
to the Lenskis' summer cottage on the Cape, and I was planning to join them for a vacation *en famille* during the month of
August.

My heart leapt. Katrina and I had been working together for six months—interrupted by her trips for *Life*,
which were often several weeks long—yet she had never spoken of her father. Even if we were far from discovering what
was truly going on in her unconscious life, we had already
been successful in relieving most of her insomnia. As a result,
her sleep was yielding some rich dream material.

"Yes, go on."

"My father's hands were covered with blood. We were digging a trench in the backyard—"

"A trench?"

"You know, a tunnel, the way children do, in the dirt—"

"But you said *trench*." I push her.

Silence. I have lost her.

"What did you call your father?"

She has been unable to speak her father's name, if she indeed knows it.

"What do you mean?"

"Did you call him Father? Papa? Daddy?"

She shrugged her shoulders and swiveled around to glare at me. Clearly I was irritating her with these seemingly irrelevant questions.

"I don't remember." She slumped back down on the couch.

I let her stew for a few moments. Katrina Volk's three favorite words were *I don't remember*.

"Go on with the dream—"

"At the foot of the trench were three birds. Two were emaciated, so thin they could barely stand. They were shivering, and I was afraid they would fall into the hole. The third bird was big and fat, and hopped the whole way around the perimeter of the trench, kicking bits of dirt inside."

She stopped. Moments of silence ticked by.

"You have nothing to say?"

Her voice was reedy with frustration, and for a few more minutes I said nothing, but then I asked a question.

"What did you feel when you awoke from the dream?"

"A phrase was rolling around my head."

"What phrase was that?"

"*Deutsche Christen.*"

I drew my breath sharply.

"What does that mean to you?"

Deutsche Christen translates into "German Christians," a civilian group that fought alongside the Nazis for domination of the church. Its members were avowed Nazis. The children of its members were usually card-carrying Hitler Youth.

"It means nothing," Katrina said vaguely.

She rolled over on the couch, onto her stomach. Her skirt was bunched up, her bare legs clearly visible. Didn't she know? Couldn't she feel it? She stared up at me, the almond-shaped eyes, the tangle of dark curls. I wondered if she had been blond as an infant—platinum hair surrounding her face in a perfect Aryan halo.

"Why don't we talk about *you*, Dr. Grossman? What did you dream about last night?"

I looked at her mildly, straining with every muscle in my body to appear at ease. After all, she was hardly the first female patient to be flirtatious with me. Even perfect strangers, women on the street found me attractive in those days. I was wiry, tightly coiled, with a strong profile and a full head of dark hair. But Katrina—Katrina unnerved me. My eyes gave me away—I blinked rapidly, as if trying to clear my vision.

"Why do you ask?"

I had begun to believe Katrina Volk had been sent to me by the ghost of Sigmund Freud. She was a psychoanalytic testing ground, an Olympian hurdle I had to cross in my quest for professional greatness. We all have patients we don't like —patients who bore us or remind us of some unpleasant aspect of ourselves. But what happens when we are faced with a patient who moves us? A patient with whom—if circumstances were slightly different—we might fall in love?

I dreamt about you, Katrina.

Of course I didn't say that—but it would have been true. After all, Katrina was only eight years younger than I. Had I met her on the subway, or at the opening of an exhibition, we might have ended up sitting across a café table from one another, rather than this analytic setting with its unbreakable set of rules. Here, I could hide behind a cloak of propriety. The mild expression, the pad, my own supervisor's advice running through my head: when in doubt, when in the throes of countertransference, take a few steps back. Let the patient take the lead.

"Why do you want to know? What do you think I dream about?" I asked, nauseated by my own gavotte. My questions were all well within reason—textbook appropriate —but I knew there was a deep, growing subtext between us, words beneath words which were beginning to buzz so loudly both of us could hear them.

She smiled as she arranged herself on the couch, cross-legged, though our session wasn't nearly over. She reached up and gathered her hair to one side of her neck, twirling it around and around in a dark spiral. A few strands escaped, curls framing her face.

"I think—"

She trailed off, looking down.

"Go on." I prodded.

"I think you dream about me," she said softly, meeting my eyes levelly.

My heart skipped a beat.

"What is your fantasy?" My voice sounded constricted to my own ears.

Time slowed down over the next few minutes. I have played and replayed each second—oh, that I had handled myself differently!—so many times in my life that I can freeze the frame at any point and torture myself with each image. Her hands shook as she unbuttoned the first button of her thin, white cotton blouse, then the second and third, until the lace of her brassiere was clearly visible.

"What are you doing?" I choked out.

Her eyes were bright. The insanity had begun.

"Tell me you don't dream about this," she whispered. "Tell me and I'll stop."

I was mute, my voice swallowed deep in my throat.

"Underneath it all, admit you despise me—" she murmured, oblivious, as she kept unbuttoning each mother-of-pearl button until, with a single shrug, she was sitting on my couch in her skirt, sandals, and bra.

"Why—do you think I despise you?" I asked desperately.

Don't look, Grossman. Just don't look.

I stared resolutely at the venetian blinds turned down against the late-afternoon sun. A single shaft of light slanted across the room, hitting Katrina's bare stomach. I tried to keep my eyes off her—but just like a wreck along the side of a highway, a beautiful half-naked woman cannot be passed without a glance.

"I saw the pictures of your family," she responded. "In Berlin. I recognized Berlin."

She reached behind her to unclasp her bra.

"They were killed, weren't they. You know what I am," she continued. "You know who my father was."

Her bra fell to the floor.

I closed my eyes and vowed to keep them closed. In quick succession I saw the front doors of the Institute slamming shut, the horror on my supervisor's face, and Ruthie— Ruthie's big brown eyes widening into permanent bitterness.

"Get dressed, Miss Volk," I said quietly.

"My father's name was Hermann Muensch," she said, her voice a child's singsong. "From what I can gather, he was like *this*"—I could picture her holding up two crossed fingers —"with Joseph Goebbels."

If this revelation had come during the course of an analytic session, I would have considered it a major breakthrough. But coming as it did, from a half-naked woman on my couch, it felt to me as if Goebbels himself had infiltrated my inner sanctum—as if he had sent an Aryan angel of death, who turned my own fantasies inside-out and used them to destroy me.

I heard her moving off the couch. The room was spinning beneath my closed eyes, a swirling vertigo. I prayed that she was bending over, picking up her bra, gathering her blouse. Instead, I saw a darkening, a shadow standing in front of me, blocking the light.

"Look at me," she whispered.

"No, Katrina."

I thought if I kept my eyes closed, if I refused to see, the situation might still be redeemable.

"Please—"

Was she offering herself to me as some sort of humble sacrifice? Her pale white flesh, unblemished perfection, an antidote to her father's war crimes?

"Miss Volk," I forced myself to say slowly—as much to myself as to her—"our time is up. We'll talk about this tomorrow."

I calmed myself by imagining our three o'clock session the following day. She would lie on the couch, I would sit in my chair and explore the transference: *Why do you think I despise you? What is your fantasy of making love with me? Tell me your dreams.*

I felt something soft, impossibly soft against my cheek. I opened my mouth in spite of myself, her nipple stiff, poisonous, tantalizing against my tongue.

A sound escaped from my mouth—a moan, primal and male—and I snapped out of it. I grabbed the edge of my chair and pushed myself up, eyes springing open. She stood before me, naked from the waist up. Those beautiful, rounded breasts had not yet been formed during the years she had done her best to repress, when she herself undoubtedly took part in the human snake, a parade of towheaded, flat-chested children marching through the streets of Berlin, singing *Deutschland, Deutschland, über alles!* at the top of their fluty little voices.

My buzzer rang.

"Put your clothes on, Miss Volk," I croaked.

She stared at me, unmoving.

"I said get dressed."

She didn't budge.

"I will be waiting by the door," I said stiffly. The colors of my office had all intensified in the past five minutes—the reds becoming burgundy, brown turning deep and rich, the light through the window blindingly white.

She bent down to gather her things, breasts swaying, and I was filled with sadistic urges: I wanted to whip her bare back, to bend her over and spank her—and more. My eyes traveled hungrily over her pale shoulders, her narrow rib cage. She had ruined me in a single moment.

She walked to the door. Her cheeks were flushed, blouse misbuttoned, lacy brassiere stuffed into her portfolio. She stood on tiptoe and brushed her lips against my cheek.

Her eyes shone with tears.

"I meant you no harm," she whispered.

I stared straight ahead and waited, holding my breath as she moved past me into the waiting room.

YOUR MOTHER CALLED that night, from the Lenskis' home on Cape Cod. Her voice was more joyful than I had heard it in months —undoubtedly something to do with being away from me. I could almost picture her bundled in a blanket beside a roaring fire, her hair wild from the salt air, you fast asleep in her arms. You were both exhausted, she told me, from clam-digging that afternoon—such a goyisheh activity!—and afterward, there had been a clambake on the beach.

"How is he?" I asked.

"Beautiful—I swear he's grown an inch in two weeks—"

"Wake him up," I said.

"No, Sol—I'll never be able to get him back to sleep!"

"Just this once," I pleaded. I needed to whisper into your tiny ear, to hear you breathing into the receiver.

Ruthie put the phone down with a sigh, and I heard her rustling, cooing at you, then the sweet sound of your tired giggles.

"Here he is!" I could hear Ruthie say. "Here's Daddy!"

And I whispered nonsense into your ear, I tickled you with my voice. "Da—" I could have sworn you spurted out, "Da—" as if my absence had somehow made me clearer to you.

I told you I loved you more than the moon and the stars. I told you I would do anything for you—that I would watch over you that night and every night as long as you lived.

Of course you could not yet speak, much less understand. Still, did you know, Daniel? Did you know even then, that I was lying?

THE FOLLOWING AFTERNOON, Katrina was late for her appointment. After my two o'clock left, I paced around my office, straightening the framed Freud letter, rearranging a volume of Kohut that was out of alphabetical order. I picked lint off the couch, replaced the tissue on which my previous patient had lain his head, then sat down for a moment, dizzy. I had a sudden flash of Katrina sitting precisely in the same spot the day before, her shoulders glowing in the late-afternoon light—and I leapt to my feet, stung.

I went to my files and pulled the one labeled *Volk.* I usually kept meticulous records of each patient, transcribing my session notes, writing my clinical impressions if not after every session, certainly once a month. Why was her folder so thin? How had I not noticed, in six months of working with her, this aberration in my work habits? I sat at my desk and stared at the near-empty folder, conscious of each revolution of the clock's second hand. I tilted the venetian blinds so I could see the street below: my heart surged with each passing cab. I needed to be forewarned of Katrina's arrival—if she was coming at all—to have the advantage of an extra few seconds to compose myself.

Volk, Katrina. Age 24. Symptoms: insomnia, self-destructive tendencies, masochism (?). Unconscious hostility/childhood repression.

My notes were scribbled on yellow legal paper. Big, loopy handwriting, a few paltry pages. Puerile, almost meaningless early observations. I closed my eyes, took a deep breath. *Help me,* I surprised myself by whispering. Whose help was I seeking? The appropriate place for me to have sought advice about this problem, my own countertransference, was in an analytic supervision. I marched dutifully to my supervisor's office each week, armed with reams of notes on patients I found troubling for one reason or another, but I always neglected to mention Katrina—the low, buzzing subtext of my life, the three syllables beneath each question, each observation. *Ka-tri-na.* I would later understand that the seeds of my own ruin had been planted months earlier. I had avoided the subject of my erotic feelings toward Katrina because I didn't wish them to be analyzed. And I didn't want them analyzed because—

A cab pulled up to the curb at the moment I picked up the phone and dialed my supervisor. *Ring.* Katrina's long legs emerged—she was wearing one of those short skirts which had just become popular with young girls—and an unwieldy camera bag was slung over her shoulder. *Ring.* She leaned forward and paid the driver, threw her head back and laughed at something he said. I watched through the tilted blinds as she stood on the sidewalk for a moment, looking around her, faltering. *Ring.* She gathered her hair in a Katrina-like gesture and twirled it into a single dark coil.

"Go away," I whispered.

I was turning into someone who talked to himself.

"Go away."

She stared right at me. It was impossible—I knew she couldn't see me hovering behind the blinds, couldn't possibly have heard me through the double-paned window—but still I felt heat rising in my cheeks.

I was flushed when I opened the door for her, and she moved quickly past me to the couch, eyes averted. She placed her camera bag on the floor, and leaned her handbag against it. She was supine before I had even reached my chair, legs stretched and crossed daintily at the ankles.

I could hear my own pulse so loudly I was sure it filled the room. *Ba-da-dum. Ba-da-dum. Ba-da-dum.* Beethoven or Wagner. A subway train clattering over the tracks. Two people rhythmically rocking, bed banging against the wall.

"A bomb explosion killed four black girls in a church down South this morning—" she began haltingly. "I may have to go fly there on assignment tonight."

I was silent. I didn't trust myself. The images imprinting themselves on my brain were violent, sexual, so vivid they seemed only a small leap away from being real. I shook my head hard, trying to wipe the thoughts clean—but instead I saw Katrina's narrow rib cage, her breast swaying above my lips, hypnotic as a pendulum. I despised myself for my fantasies.

A few moments ticked by.

"Did you hear me?" she asked.

I cleared my throat.

"Yes—I heard about it on the morning news—"

"They were just kids—the youngest was no more than four or five—"

"The same age you were when your father died—" I associated.

"This has nothing to do with me—" she interrupted. "I don't want to go on this assignment. I can't bear what's going on the South—the segregation, the riots—"

A slight tremor in her voice gave her away.

"Is this what you want to be talking about?" I asked mildly. I had regained my footing.

"It's awful! Children killed! Don't you have a heart?"

I felt a microscopic pellet at the base of my spine—the locus of my rage—explode and shoot through my bones.

"Heart?" I barked at my own torturer, the beautiful daughter of Hermann Meunsch, best friend of Joseph Goebbels. "Heart?" I repeated, almost choking on the bile of my own fury.

Found my footing, indeed! I was lost, flailing through the air between us, my long-dormant nerve endings bristing with passion in all its various mutations. I wanted to punish Katrina Volk—to tear the skin from beneath her fingernails, bury my hands deep in the nest of her hair, and pull back on her scalp until her head snapped. I wanted to bend her over my desk, yank her flimsy little skirt up, and spank her. I wanted to slap her Aryan cheeks until they were pink with shame. A lifetime of training myself to objectively follow the course of my thoughts was now failing me miserably. Every thought I followed led me to the same closed door of self-loathing.

"Yes—" she spit out, still lying down, "*heart*. You think sitting there in your judgment chair with your big fat doctorate entitles you to some special dispensation? You think whatever you've been through in your life absolves you? You've suffered enough—now you get to float above it all?"

She had taken a wild pot shot—and come close to hitting the bull's-eye. How did she know? Katrina had been my patient for six months, and it seemed she was the one with all the insight. She sounded like my own wife. *Enough with the war, Solly. You were one of the lucky ones. So what are you going to do with your luck?* Ruthie's dark eyes hovered over me in the dim, artificial light of my office, challenging, accusatory—waiting for me to trip over myself.

"Look around yourself, Dr. Grossman. Everyone has their fair share of tragedy. People are dying all over the world —the Buddhist monks in Hue who set themselves on fire, the Birmingham riots—"

"What are you really trying to say to me?" I asked.

She sat up, buried her head in her hands. My eyes traveled up the length of her legs, the rounded curve of her hunched shoulders.

"I don't know—" she said wearily, "I'm sorry. What I did yesterday—it was wrong."

"Let's talk about it."

As long as we kept talking—as long as the poison between us was shaped into language and not gesture—we would remain within the bounds of psychoanalysis.

"I felt I should give you something—something of myself—"

"A sacrifice?" I prodded.

"I suppose."

"Why?"

"The first time I ever came to see you, I made a wrong turn leaving your office and walked down the hall to the kitchen. I saw your wife and baby, and the photographs of your family in Berlin, wearing those yellow stars—"

She was looking at me, her eyes heavy, half-lidded. She had poisoned me, and now that my veins were tainted, she was confessing to the crime.

"I know where I come from," she said quietly. "I spend my life living with that."

"As do I," I responded in spite of myself, "and there's nothing you can do to change it."

With that, she hunched over and began to weep.

"I try—" she gulped. "—my photographs—"

"I know," I said gently. "I know."

Watching her shoulders heave with sobs, I was blessed with a moment of absolute clarity.

"Miss Volk"—I cleared my throat—"I am clearly not the right analyst for you. I think you would be much better off with someone whose—background—does not intersect with yours in the way mine does."

She stopped crying and was now staring at me through a tangle of hair. I heard a loud, unintelligible whisper in my head, a voice directing me urgently—giving me directions to a place I had never been.

"Today would have been our last session before my August break. I will give some thought during the break to a referral—"

I began to rise from my chair. She was rocking back and forth, like a catatonic.

"But for now," I continued, "our time is up—"

I stood by the door, trying to breathe.

Slowly, dutifully, like a child, Katrina gathered her belongings and walked toward me. She was my last patient of the day. My hand was on the doorknob, my body angled away from her—*just let her go*—and then whatever microscopic amount of resolution that was holding me together dissolved like weak glue, and suddenly she was in my arms, pressed against me—my hands raking through her hair, lips closing down on hers with a ferocity that terrified me even as it pushed me beyond all reason.

In the ensuing weeks, the question of who made that first move would become a central one. Did I pull Katrina toward me? Did she push herself against me? In the end, does it really matter? I have spent my life living with the consequences of that afternoon. You can read the newspaper accounts, if you wish—perhaps even gain access to the Institute's records. But will you ever understand, beneath the scorn you must feel for me, that I was attempting the impossible? That I was trying to rewrite history on the body of a woman?

HER BACK WAS UP AGAINST THE DOOR. I reached behind her and pressed the lock until it clicked shut—though there were no patients expected, and no one at home. She was wearing a blouse similar to the one she had worn the previous day—but this time I grabbed the collar and ripped it vertically, tiny mother-of-pearl buttons clattering across the floor, wedging themselves into the carpet where I would find them for months to come. I pushed her bra straps down, yanked her bra to her waist and bent over, hearing her backbone bang against my office door, squeezing her perfectly rounded breasts together, pushing both nipples into my mouth at the same time, biting, sucking recklessly. It would be untrue to say I didn't care about hurting her. I *did* care—I *wanted* her to cry out in pain as I fumbled with her skirt zipper, pulled it down, yanked down her panties, unzipped my own fly in a matter of seconds and pushed her across the room to the couch.

It was only once Katrina was spread-eagled across my couch that I paused to look her in the eye. She stared right back at me, her face flushed, triumphant, lips moist.

I slapped her across the face.

She smiled at me serenely. We had entered a foreign country, a neutral zone. We had only temporary visas, a one-day pass. We were travelers obeying the laws of the land.

I slapped her again.

Is this what you wanted?

I ripped her skirt off. Her clothes were in tatters. How would she ever get home? How would I ever let her leave? She lay back on the couch, legs bare, cream-colored panties loose around one ankle, lacy brassiere dangling around her waist like a belt. I was fully dressed in my suit pants, shirt, cuff links, and tie—and I undid my pants so they hung below my knees.

I turned her over and grabbed her ass. She was too beautiful, too lean, too pale and long-limbed—a card-carrying member of the Master Race. I spanked her until she was bright red, until my hand stung. I slid into her with no ceremony. She craned her head so she could watch, that dreamy smile never leaving her face. She arched toward me as I pounded myself into her, as I dove into her and drowned.

The light faded beneath the slats of the venetian blinds. It was a sultry night, the last night of my life as I knew it. On the street below, through the double-paned glass, I heard the sounds of rush hour: taxi doors slamming, footsteps marching home, dogs being walked. I grabbed onto her hair, holding it like a rope.

We rolled onto the floor with a thud. Now she was beneath me, breasts pressed against my chest, meeting each of my thrusts with a deeper one of her own. She was letting me know that I could not tame her. She turned her neck to the side, her cheek pressed against the stubble of the rug, a delicate vein throbbing. She reached a hand down to the base of my spine and stroked me with infinite tenderness.

A sound escaped my lips, a hybrid between a groan and

a wail. Tears and sweat stung my eyes as I watched the bright moral center of my existence bob like a life raft floating away from my grasp.

Harder, she whispered. Did I imagine this, or did she say it? *Harder. Don't stop, you Jewish bastard. Fuck me.*

SEVEN

LIKE A GIANT SPIDER perched atop spindly steep legs, the Theme Restaurant guards all of Los Angeles International Airport. I wonder what the theme is? A bronze plaque informs me that it's actually an architect's rendering of a spaceship, circa 1963, but that is of little help to my nauseous stomach as I take the elevator to the restaurant. I hope it isn't going to be one of those revolving deals. Instead, I step into a room which is like HoJo's with a view. From here, the runways of LAX have a strange, tentacular beauty—thank God we are not turning in circles.

The bar is empty, and I sit down. The bartender is riveted to the television, watching a frosted blond talk-show hostess try to control a panel of young white supremacists and a booing audience. They are all shouting, one louder than the next.

Go back to Africa where you all belong!

(bleep) you! How can you (bleep) believe what you're—

I content myself reading the ingredients of a packet of Equal. Whoever invented this stuff must be a wealthy sonofa-bitch.

Finally the bartender tears himself away.

"What can I get you?

I want a drink, but it's still before noon. Coffee will only speed my heart up. Okay, the hell with it. I'll have a drink with milk.

"White Russian."

He doesn't even blink—airports are time-free zones. Anybody who pays good money to hurl himself through space at supersonic speeds in thirty tons of steel deserves whatever he can get at any hour. In the distance, at the edge of an outlying runway, cranes, unmarked cars, dozens of men in maintenance uniforms work in the midday sun, scavenging like predatory animals through what's left of World 103.

I squint into the haze. The men all look the same from here. I check my watch. Quarter to twelve. Is Daniel on his way?

"You have a helluva view," I say to the bartender.

He nods solemnly, eyes back to the white supremacists.

"Saw the whole thing." Does he think I'm connected to the crash too? I wear the clothes of a survivor wherever I go?

"Tell me," I prod, half-curious, half killing time. After all, what more do I need to know? I've seen it on television, I've seen it in person. The faces of my fellow passengers on last night's expedition to the crash site flip through my head, one by one, a slide show of grief. Where are they now? Signing papers at the morgue? Shipping body bags back?

"I'm a vet," he says, grabbing the silver shaker and a carton of milk at the same time, and topping off the sickening mixture of vodka and Kahlúa. He leans over the bar as if to tell me a secret. For a moment I think he's talking about animals—why would an animal doctor be tending bar in a makeshift spaceship at LAX?—then I realize he means, of course, that he fought in a war, probably Vietnam, judging from his age. As it turns out, this is one species of human with whom I have had little contact. Vets don't generally visit $150-an-hour analysts on Riverside Drive. Better to see someone whose hand is quick with a scrip for lithium or Halcion.

"I've seen a grenade explode in a guy's face," says the bartender as I sip my drink. "I've seen men step on land mines and spurt up like geysers—"

He looks at me closely to see if I'm getting it. I take a gulp of my White Russian and it spreads through my chest like honey.

"But I ain't never seen nothing like that crash."

I look down at my glass and realize it's empty. Never in my life have I had a drink before lunchtime. I push it toward him. The booze seems to be acting as a tranquilizer, keeping my racing heart under control.

This time he pours me a double, a healthier splash of vodka with a brown cap of Kahlúa and a little milk. I can feel him assessing me the way a new patient might—checking my clothes, my shoes, my watch, my absence of a wedding band.

"You know somebody who was on that plane?" Almost an accusation.

"No."

"You just get here, or are you going someplace?"

"Neither."

He cocks his head.

"So what's your story?"

"I don't have a story."

"Come on," he says, glancing once again at the television. The talk-show hostess is now interviewing parents of white supremacists.

What, I'm going to tell a bartender—an airport bartender at that—my life story? He must be joking. Who would want to tend bar in the middle of an airport, where you never get the same customer twice? Or maybe that's the beauty of it.

He's still looking at me.

"You're not okay," he says flatly, as if telling me something I already know.

"Yes."

"Yes, what? Yes, you're not okay?"

Daniel, where are you?

By now, the Kahlúa and vodka have separated and my White Russian looks like an iced coffee. I gulp it down, then slap a twenty on the bar.

"That ought to cover me," I say. "How about another for the road."

Now that's a sentence I've never uttered before. It's a morning of nevers. Never drink during the day. Never talk to bartenders. Never speak in movie-land clichés.

"Sorry." He shakes his head. "No can do."

"Excuse me?"

He points to two signs framed on the side of the bar. The first warns pregnant women that alcohol can cause birth defects. The second forbids restaurant employees to serve customers who already seem inebriated.

Now I really need another one. My nerves are jangled, my hands are shaking with fear.

"Sir, I assure you I am not inebriated."

Inebriated sloshes out of my mouth, syllables slurred. Is that how the word came into being? As a sort of litmus test for drunks?

"Sorry," he says.

We stare at each other. In his eyes, I am seeing the opacity of someone who once killed, now works in an airport bar and watches "Oprah" all day. We are the only two people in the bar, but the noise is deafening. Television. Jets. I consider pleading with him, telling him the truth—but why?

The gridlike pattern of the carpet weaves before me as I put one shiny black shoe in front of the other and walk to the window, my left leg dragging slightly. True, I am slightly woozy—but drunk I am not. Perhaps I am just giddy, high on adrenaline. The grid scatters as I stumble, then find my balance.

"Careful there," calls the bartender, who is watching me with interest, having turned his attention from daytime television to real-time soap opera.

I am suddenly uncomfortable. My armpits are damp. I stare out the window; I cannot focus. I see a jumbo jet rolling down a runway. I blink and it is aloft, and the crabgrass along the sides of the runway seems wavy, like some hot summer dream. Can it have gotten so hot so quickly? I hear bells in my head, the persistent *ding* of elevator doors opening, but I am afraid to turn around.

"Excuse me?"

My heart is in my mouth. If I open my lips it will come spurting out, a throbbing mass of blood.

"I think you asked to see me?"

I turn slowly, head bowed. A pair of shoes is speaking to me—cordovan, well-tooled, rubber-soled shoes attached to a pair of wrinkled khaki pants. My eyes travel up the khakis, past a brown leather belt with an old silver buckle, ringless hands, up a white cotton shirt with a coffee stain between the second and third buttons. The pounding in my chest seems to have slowed. I raise my eyes, skimming over two Bic pens in a shirt pocket, sleeves rolled over pale forearms, and into a warped mirror. The eyes, the nose, the chin, the lips—are mine. Mine! Last night, I must have been too far off to see it. And now, if I could just reach out and trace his jaw, the smooth determined Grossman chin with its tiny cleft—as if it is my own father's hands cupping my face. A trace of Ruthie in his forehead, a wrinkled knot of consternation—what is he seeing? Does he see his future in my past? I imagine all of them—Meyer, Mama, Ruthie, my own blessed parents— looking down at us, frozen.

He is looking at me quizzically, my son.

"What can I do for you?" he asks.

"Daniel—"

He frowns at my presumptive use of his first name.

"Yes?"

"Come sit with me a moment."

"I'm sorry—do I know you?"

"Please."

Like a guide dog, I shepherd him to a corner booth, as

far as possible from the bartender and his white supremacists. He trails me warily. I am conscious of his footsteps behind me, padding along the carpet. Now I am stone-cold sober, and my mind is racing. How do I say it? What do I say? Do I ease my way into the subject or blurt it out at once? For all my years of dreaming, I have not rehearsed this moment—perhaps I never believed it would come.

We sit opposite each other, me on a banquette, him facing the wreck. The bartender begins to walk over to us, but I shoot him a look so daunting he backs away. Daniel looks at me expectantly, drumming his fingers.

"Is there some reason for this? What's your business?"

Monkey business. There's no business like show business. None of your business.

"My—"

The staccato rhythm against the table sends me deep into an atavistic jungle, my father's fingers against the linoleum kitchen table in Stuyvesant Town, my grandfather standing at the front door in Berlin, waiting, fingers itching against the wooden frame—my throat closes up. My mother, father, aunts, uncles, cousins—all gone, sunk like the heavy chain of an anchor—and now this rumpled blue-eyed boy with the sagging shoulders of a Grossman, bearer of a weight he can't possibly understand.

I toss him a ball, a globe the size of the world. *Catch this, boychik!*

I clear my throat.

"My name is Solomon Grossman."

He blinks rapidly, says nothing.

"Does my name mean anything to you?"

"No, I'm sorry—should it?"

He is holding a coin in his hands, flipping it back and forth between his palms. His hands are graceful, fingers sensuous, but his cuticles are bitten raw. There is a white line on his wrist where a watch should be—a pale band of skin like a hospital bracelet encircling his wrist.

"I'm your father."

I blurt it out.

His hands stop moving, fingers stop drumming, eyes stop blinking. Everything is still. His pupils jiggle almost imperceptibly as if he has been jolted from the inside—if I were not trained in such matters I would not notice.

He opens and closes his mouth.

"Here, let me get you a drink," I say.

"No," he mouths, but no sound comes out. He looks at me for a split second, then his eyes dart away. I notice a small scar on the side of his neck—a burn, perhaps, or an accident with a razor. What other scars have marked my son? I want to tear off his shirt and examine him under a bright light.

"How—?"

"I saw you on television. The instant I saw you I knew —and then I flew from New York—"

His eyes close into slits, and for a moment he looks like his maternal grandfather.

"I don't believe you."

I smile at him gently. For years I have arranged my smile in front of the mirror, adjusting my face until it reflected just the right degree of warmth. But this is a smile I haven't felt on my face in decades; it begins deep in my chest and spreads up through my throat, warming it like whiskey, then ends on my lips.

"Just look," I say. "Just look at me."

I had wondered how I would prove to Daniel that I was his father. He is a detective, after all. I had thought about bringing evidence—a 1963 photograph of the two of us, a copy of his birth certificate before the second half of his surname was sliced away—but now it has dawned on me that my own face is all I need. Over the years, I admit, a few doubts wormed their way into my mind: I didn't actually *see* the doctor inject Ruthie. What if he dropped the test tube on the floor, glass shattering, sperm hitting the air? What if my thirty years of longing had been for the product of Ruth Lenski and the semen of some Irish Catholic graduate student?

Slowly Daniel lifts his eyes to meet mine and the mirror wavers between us. I see him take me in. He is looking into his own physical future, there is no mistaking it—the lines which will one day ring his eyes, the single crease in the center of his forehead, the slight sagging beneath the chin.

"I thought you were dead."

"Ah."

"They told me you died when I was a year old."

His voice is constricted, narrowed into a whistle.

I am silent.

Those sons of bitches.

"I didn't believe them—when I was in high school I even went looking for my father—but I didn't get anywhere."

"Yes. I thought that might have been the case."

"Why?" He rakes a hand through his hair violently. I want to stop him, grab his wrist, but I don't dare.

"Why would they tell me you were dead?"

He is shrinking before my eyes, the years peeling off, one by one, and I see him as a young adult, a pain-in-the-ass college student, a sullen adolescent, a bright and shining boy.

He presses back against his chair, as far away from me as possible. His shoulders are hunched, shuddering. Across his forehead march a thousand questions. I see them as if they were branded there, and each one begins with a single word: *why? why? why?*

"Why did they tell me you were dead?" he asks again. A question so bizarre it bears repeating.

"You'll have to ask your mother that," I answer softly.

"She died six months ago."

The words hit me like a dull weapon, the pain taking a moment to register.

"Ruth is dead?" I ask dumbly.

"Car accident."

"My God."

I was not expecting this. I had not even considered—I bury my head in my hands. Everything was going so smoothly. I was doing so well. *Ruthie—dead?* I have not spoken with her in thirty years. Still, I assumed she would outlive me, pickled and preserved by modern cosmetical science.

My brain begins to swirl.

Mustn't let him see—

I lift myself up. The room is spinning, planes lined up on the runway colliding in my head—

"Please. Can't I get you a drink?" I try again.

"Is what you're saying that *you'd* like a drink?" Daniel asks.

"Vodka straight," I say, digging into my pocket.

He holds up a hand.

"Please, allow me," he says with no discernible irony.

I watch as he walks over to the bar. His brown hair falls just over the edges of his ears.

My stomach turns over.

"Daniel!" I call.

He whips around, as if his own name is a shock.

"I'm going to use the men's room," I say. "I'll be right back."

His eyes widen—in panic, perhaps? Has he always imagined his father calling out to him from a distance—*I'll be back*—the hollow lie echoing in his dreams?

I make a quick trip to the men's room. My skin has bleached even whiter since I last looked in a mirror, and my face seems to have sagged, loose flesh hanging from my jaw. I bend over at the sink, splashing myself with cupped palms full of cold water.

Blood rushes to my head, my knees buckle. I fall to the floor as if in slow motion. A soft gray fog rolls in, blown from the mouth of my deceased ex-wife. The industrial tile is cold as I hit my head against the sink's pedestal, almost waking me from my faint—almost, but not quite. I am bathed in clouds which mutate like computer-generated sketches of criminals— Ruthie's face becomes Meyer's, then turns into the coarse peasant features of my own grandparents. I see a landfill, a mountain of crumbling tombstones, Daniel rummaging through each slab, up to his elbows in dust. He runs his fingers over names and dates like a blind man reading braille. And then, with great embarrassment, I see myself splayed on the cold tile of the bathroom floor as I return to consciousness.

God—please not—

A muttered curse, then a hand on my forehead, resting there for a split second like a blessing. Two strong arms beneath my armpits, hoisting me up. I am limp as a rag doll, my right side as weak as my left. I stare into the mirror, beneath the harsh fluorescent lights, at two twin faces, young and old. The faces go in and out of focus, undulating, keeping time with the pounding in my head. This wasn't quite how I imagined the aesthetics of our father-son reunion.

"What's happened?" I rasp.

"I don't know—you were taking a long time—I began to wonder where you were—"

"Get me out of here—"

"Can you walk?"

"Of course I can walk!"

He lets go of me, and I begin to crumble before he grabs on to me again, his chest against mine, a perversely clinical hug. It has been a lifetime since I've felt a rib cage pressed against mine and I am surprised by his frailty—he is holding me up, yet I feel I could break him in two.

"I'm taking you to the hospital," he mutters.

"No!" I howl in his ear.

"But you're clearly ill!"

"Please—I just got nervous, is all."

"I can't deal with this—it's a fucking disaster area out there and I have work to do. You picked a helluva time to drop in on my life—"

"I didn't pick the time, Daniel. The time picked me."

"What's that supposed to mean?"

He is holding me by the shoulders.

"I didn't know how to find you."

"How is that possible? Where were you?"

Our words echo off the lima-bean-green tiles of the men's room. He backs away from me and leans against the sink, leaving me unsteady on my feet.

"I live in New York. Where I've always been. In the house you lived in as a baby," I respond gravely.

His eyes are alarmingly bright. Has he had flashes all his life, fragments of memory—a dark staircase, two moon-faces peering down at his baby self in a crib, a rough stubbled cheek brushing against his own? Has he been plagued by dreams of a place he can't remember, raised voices in a corridor receding, fading, a bedroom door slammed shut? Or perhaps he has repressed all of it? Has my son visited an analyst's couch? He would have needed a good one.

"Did you know," I ask, "that your name was changed?"

He shakes his head no.

"My name is Solomon Grossman," I say slowly, "and the name you were born with was Daniel Grossman."

"Daniel Grossman," he mumbles to himself.

He wheels around.

"I don't believe you—why wouldn't it be on my birth certificate, then?"

"Your grandfather had his ways," I shrug.

He is silent. Unless Meyer had radically mellowed with age, the unethical ways in which he used his power could not be denied.

"Why did they lie to me? Why did they change my name? Why didn't you try to find me?"

His questions are like pieces to an intricate puzzle scattered all over the floor between us. I know we will get nowhere until at least the corners are filled in.

"Look, why don't we go somewhere quiet to talk?" I ask him.

"Not until you answer my questions."

"Must I do it standing in the men's room of an airport bar?"

"Well, you should have thought of that before you just decided to pop up in the middle of an investigation."

He folds his arms. Ah, you stubborn Grossman genes go marching on. Throw in a dash of Lenski entitlement and you end up with quite a frothy recipe.

"At least, let's go back to the bar—"

"You don't still want your vodka—!"

Actually, I do still want my vodka. My mouth waters at the very notion. I can see it, languishing on the table, beads of moisture forming around the lip of the glass—but I don't dare. It would be like tossing lighter fluid down my gut. Besides, what would he think? That his father is a world-class Jewish drunk?

"Of course not—but I need to sit down—"

Lie down is more like it.

I feel a steady stream of sweat trickling down my forehead. It's hot in the men's room, but not so hot that I should be sweating like a stuck pig. I glance in the mirror and for a split second I think I can see through the back of my head to the paper towel dispenser on the wall behind me. I have finally become transparent. Can Daniel see through me? I whirl around and confront the back wall, then turn to my left and face Daniel.

"Is anything wrong?" my voice trembles.

Palpitations and headaches are one thing, but when I start seeing clear through my own head, I get worried.

"What do you mean?"

"Does anything about me seem—strange?"

He cracks a small smile.

"Everything about you seems strange."

We stand, warily eyeing each other. Where to go from here? It has been more or less firmly established that we are related by blood. The mirror is our proof, our witness. And—so what? For all intents and purposes, I have not been his father since he was a year old. Do I have any right to him? If I reached out and touched him, would he jump away? Women are better at this sort of thing. A mother and daughter would know how to have a proper reunion—they would meet under the clock at The Plaza or at a softly lit café. None of these urinals and fluorescent lights. How would Ruthie have done it? Not that Ruthie would ever have found herself in this position. I'm sure she was in perfect control of her life until the moment she went crashing through the windshield of her car.

"What happened to your mother?" I ask softly.

"Like you really care," he snorts.

"I do care, Daniel."

Daniel, Daniel—his name slides off my tongue as if I've been saying it all my life.

"Yeah, okay."

"Whatever else, I loved your mother."

"Head-on collision. Drunk driver," he spits out, one sharp bone after another.

"Had she remarried?"

"More than once."

Why should this surprise me? I was only the beginning of Ruthie's rebellion. Who were the others? I can only imagine—did she marry a goy, some poor golf-playing, gold-digging Roman Catholic Republican? Maybe even a *shvartzer*? Meyer and Mama should have realized what a good bargain they had with me. I was Jewish, white, with a string of initials after my name.

"She ended up spun into the divider on the Saw Mill," he says.

He is biting the edge of his thumb, which is already chewed raw. His nails are all bitten into the pink, puckered and brand-new like a baby's skin.

I close my eyes.

"I'm sorry."

"Shit happens."

"It must have been very difficult for you—"

"Actually, I've gotten quite used to seeing wrecks."

I am having visions—I cannot stop them—an ancient slide projector has imbedded itself on the tissue of my inner eye and is flashing black-and-white images, each more horrific than the next. The images are stark, utterly devoid of sentiment though beautifully composed—as if Katrina Volk had documented my life and the lives of those I have loved. I see Ruthie's mangled head against a broken steering wheel, blood dribbling from the corner of her mouth—crimson, like the shade of her favorite Elizabeth Arden lipstick. I see a car—some Nazi-mobile—with its hood pushed in like an accordion, steam billowing into the Connecticut night. But worst of all, I see my son, standing like a statue in the flashing blue strobe of a police car as his mother's body is poured onto a stretcher, then covered with a white sheet.

Did he think she was joining me, then, his long-deceased father? Did the thought flash through his mind that he was now an orphan? Did he imagine his two parents merging, blending into one another as we were never able to do in life? Where did he bury Ruth—at the feet of her father? For centuries to come, Meyer Lenski will be stomping on his daughter's head.

"I would like—" I stop, rocks in my throat.

He now has tears streaming down his face. Another Grossman trait—when we cry, the rivers of Germany flow from our eyes.

"I would like to try—"

"Yes—" says my son, reaching out a hand, grasping my arm. I feel the heat of his palm through my shirt. "Let's go someplace quiet to talk."

EIGHT

THE TWENTY-FOUR HOURS in which my life fell apart began
with a Saturday morning phone call. They purposefully chose
to call my home and not my office—a hostile gesture if there
ever was one. I was asleep on my office couch when Ruthie
came padding down the hall and rapped sharply on the door.

"Solomon! Telephone!"

I turned to look at my clock—the all-important analytic
clock, which converts time instantly into dollars—and shook
myself awake. It was just before seven-thirty, early for a
weekend call. I groggily opened the door to Ruthie's back,
already turned away from me, and followed her down the
hall to the phone in the kitchen.

"Who is it?" I asked the back of her head.

"Handelman," she grumbled. "I was in the middle of
feeding Daniel."

"Sorry, dear heart."

"What could he possibly want at seven-thirty in the morning?"

She turned around, flipped her hair at me, dark eyes flashing. The front of her robe hung open.

The warning bells in my head had not yet begun to ring. What had happened between Katrina Volk and myself in the privacy—indeed sanctity—of my own office seemed to be somehow inviolate, utterly beyond the realm of public scrutiny. When the door to my office clicked shut behind a patient, my office became a world within the world, a remote island where the unacceptable was accepted, the unimaginable imagined—and finally, the impossible possible.

"Hello?"

"Good morning, Solomon," the dry voice of Joseph Handelman, *über*-analyst, director of the Institute, crackled over the line.

"Joseph, to what do I owe this honor—"

"We need to see you this afternoon," said Handelman.

Something in the simple single syllable—the pronoun *we* —made my stomach turn over.

"What's up?" I tried to keep my tone breezy.

"Three o'clock," he ignored my question, "in the conference room."

I glanced at Ruthie, who was once again feeding Daniel. Her head was leaned back against a window molding, her neck smooth and white. A small vein throbbed in time with Daniel's sucking. Her eyes were closed. I knew she was listening.

"We're supposed to visit my in-laws this afternoon," I said weakly.

"Grossman, this is not optional. Do you understand?"

Handelman's tone was utterly devoid of the fatherly warmth I had come to expect from him. I had always been one of his favorites.

"Joseph, can't you tell me what's—"

The phone went dead. I kept talking.

"Oh, I see, I see," I chuckled heartily. "Yes, of course I understand. I'll be there. No problem."

A *click.*

"Looking forward to it. Good-bye, Joseph."

Dial tone.

I placed the receiver back on its hook. My hands were trembling, and I felt as if I was about to lose control of my bowels. My life, quite literally, flashed before my eyes. In quick order, I saw the stone archways of the Rykestrasse in Berlin (seen from the vantage point of a boy no taller than a fire hydrant); my thick letter of acceptance into the Yeshiva doctoral program; my chance meeting with the lovely Ruth Lenski; the Victorian couch Ruthie found at an antique store and had reupholstered in burgundy velvet for my graduation present; the first time I scrawled Ph.D. next to my name. (My son's name is abbreviated. He shortened Grossman, and I lengthened it with the three classiest letters in the alphabet.)

How had they found out?

Only one answer was possible. I saw Katrina Volk's thighs open up, the symmetrical pink mouth between them moist and gaping, swallowing my whole life in one gulp.

"What was that all about?" Ruthie shifted Daniel from one breast to the other.

"Oh, they're planning a surprise party for Bernheim," I said casually. "They need my help this afternoon."

"But, Solomon, you promised!"

"Nothing I can do about it," I shrugged, blasé as could be.

"They act like they own you," Ruth fumed.

"Ah, but they do," I murmured. "They do."

My darling wife did not understand the concept of being owned, having always been on the other side of it. Besides, how could the Institute own me, when she had paid retail?

"But what will I tell Mama and Daddy? They'll be so disappointed."

"Tell them you have a husband who works."

"On a Saturday," she said flatly.

"Ruthie, I'm warning you. I don't want to talk about it."

Lately, I had been issuing ultimatums with increasing frequency. *I don't want to talk about it. I'm warning you. I mean it. Be careful.* What, exactly, was I threatening? I had absolutely no intention of walking out the door, leaving behind my wife, my child, my soundproofed office. It is now painfully clear that this is exactly what I should have done. A marriage crumbles by degrees. First a seed is planted in your heart, a single, fleeting thought: *why—I don't love this person. I don't even like this person*, an unfamiliar voice will quietly insist, but you brush the voice aside, you shout it down with your own indefatigable desire for the status quo.

One day, there is the voice. *I don't love her.* A week later, there is a smell you never noticed before, a scent you find mildly repulsive. The way she kisses begins to irritate you—

her soft tongue flops like a dead fish in your mouth. A month later, you push your chair back from the breakfast table and begin screaming like a madman because she's chewing her breakfast cereal too loudly, smacking her lips. Is she trying to drive you out of your mind?

Perhaps if I had divorced Ruthie, painful as it might have been, the incident, as it came to be referred to at the Institute, might never have come to pass. Maybe if I had been able to recognize my unhappiness, it would not have taken its own shape and boomeranged against me. I might even have been able to work through my feelings, countertransference with Katrina. She would simply have been my three o'clock patient.

Fat chance.

LATER THAT MORNING, I told Ruthie I was taking you for a walk in Riverside Park. I didn't bother with your stroller, just hoisted you in my arms. She didn't say a word. She was still fuming at my afternoon appointment. I remember she was sitting on a window seat in the den, framed by the dappled light filtering through the trees, an intricate piece of needlepoint in her lap. She jabbed her needle quickly, methodically, not even looking up as we walked out the door.

You were getting to be a chubby little thing, almost too heavy to carry, but still I held you in the crook of one arm as I walked to a pay phone a few blocks down Broadway. I kept turning and looking over my shoulder, paranoid, afraid I was being followed. You were having a grand time as we whirled around once, twice, three times before we stopped at a phone booth and squeezed inside.

You loved to be close to me, Daniel. I know there is little

meaning in telling you this now—perhaps it is even destructive—but I cannot forget your arms clasped around my neck, the way you stared up at me as I dialed the seven digits connecting me to Katrina Volk.

"Hello?"

"Katrina?"

"Yes?"

"This is Solomon Grossman."

Click.

I fumbled for another dime, then dialed again.

"Hello?" This time her voice was sharp, guarded.

"Katrina, don't hang up," I said quickly. "I need to know if—"

"Dr. Grossman," she said, "I have been instructed not to speak with you. You should know that I am tape-recording this conversation."

I dropped the receiver and banged my head against the glass of the phone booth. Was she catching that on her tape recorder? I let out a howl like a madman. Do you remember, anywhere deep in the place where you retain your early childhood? Do you remember the sound of my head banging against the glass as you laughed and laughed, thinking it was all a game?

IT WAS EARLY SEPTEMBER, just after Yom Kippur, as I recall. New York was at the tail end of a brutally hot summer, the light harsh and flat as I made my way over to the Institute. At the beginning of the week, I had watched through the window of my air-conditioned office as Jews *shvitzing* in their woolen finery walked down Riverside toward their little *shtiebels*, tiny synagogues on the Upper West Side. Men wore dark suits despite the heat—the Orthodox ones wore sneakers. The women, determined to wear their new hats in the ninety-degree sun, patted beads of perspiration on their powdered upper lips, plumed feathers wilting.

I had decided to boycott synagogue that year, much to Ruthie's dismay. I chose to remain home rather than attend the grand services at the Park Avenue Synagogue with the Lenski clan. I could not bear to recite the list of sins, to ask God's mercy for an offense for which I could not forgive myself. *Katrina Volk.* Hers was a name which should not even be thought—much less uttered—within the sacred walls of a shul.

SO THIS WAS IT, I thought bitterly as I circled the Institute at a few minutes before three o'clock, my undershirt sticking to my chest beneath the crisp white cotton button-down and tweed blazer I had chosen for the occasion. I glanced at the sky. Somewhere up there, God had just finished sealing the fate of each Jew for the following year. I had skipped out on the Day of Atonement, and now God was forsaking me. I had dressed for my own execution. Dignity under duress. My heart pounded in time with my feet. Three beats for every step I took. *One*-two-three. *Two*-two-three: a death waltz. As far as I was concerned, my feet could just carry me away, as far away as possible from this ominous command performance.

I have been instructed not to speak with you. The sound of Katrina's voice—dignified, measured, Germanic—echoed in my ears. Who instructed her? Who knew about the single afternoon we spent together in my office—the afternoon which stretched into evening, and on into dawn—which ended only with my pathetic suggestion that she had better leave before my first patient arrived?

We had christened almost every room in my house, Katrina and I. I had her on the kitchen floor, on the living room sofa, even—God help me—on the window seat in Daniel's nursery. The only room that remained off limits was my marital bedroom, and only because I imagined that Ruthie, upon her return from the Cape, would find a piece of bra strap, a single strand of impossibly curly black hair, and hold up the evidence with a curious, disbelieving look in her eye. Even in the face of hard proof, I would probably have been able to talk my way out of it. After all, I wasn't the type to have pushed Katrina Volk against the windowsill of the living room, her bare ass pressed against the glass clearly visible to anyone bothering to look. I didn't seem like a man who would kneel before her in front of the full-length mirror in the hallway and force her to watch herself as I buried my face between her thighs. No, the mild-mannered, meticulous Solomon Grossman could not possibly be the psychoanalytic monster who spent the second-to-last night in July saying good-bye to his favorite patient—good-bye to her breasts! Good-bye to the curve of her waist! Good-bye to the black forest of her cunt—good-bye, good-bye!

No, Solomon Grossman, Ph.D., would have been asleep in his own bed, I determined as I rang the Institute's doorbell. Asleep and dreaming his super-analyzed dreams.

I was buzzed into the doors of the Institute and dazedly waited in the marble foyer as if I had not been buzzed in countless times before—I had been approaching the day where I might even have been given a key!—as if I might be a patient and not an analyst. I stood there like a patient—nervous, full of dread as the magic carpet of psychoanalysis unfurled before me, intricate in its twists and turns, utterly unfathomable.

On this early autumn Saturday two days after Yom Kippur, the place was nearly shut down. I cleared my throat and heard the sound echo off the mansion's cavernous ceiling. The ornate staircase twisted up like a half-grin to the second-floor offices and conference room where I assumed Handelman and his henchmen were waiting. I knew I should walk upstairs. I knew it was time, they were expecting me. Instead, I crossed the foyer and headed toward a bulletin board where notices of general interest were posted.

Winter Berkshires rental. Close to skiing. Three bedrooms. Perfect for family vacation. Reasonably priced—start planning Christmas early! Call KL4-5526.

Siamese cat missing. Answers to "Sasha." Please contact Mrs. Conway in the front office. Reward.

There were people out there who were planning winter vacations and posting notices about lost cats. The fine line between ordinary life and permanent exile can be crossed in a single instant. It is there, invisible like a trip wire, every minute of every day. One day you're going skiing with your family, the next you're lying in the hospital, paralyzed from the neck down. One day you're looking for your cat, the next you're finding a lipstick-stained hankie in your husband's pants pocket. *Rat-tat-tat.*

Heavy footsteps toward the door. Handelman's bald head loomed, his belly preceding him.

"All right, Solomon. Come in."

A sea of pasty, solemn faces. I did a quick head count. Around the conference table were all the senior analysts at the Institute, except for Elizabeth Zimmer, the faculty's token woman, who had just given birth the previous week. Thirteen in all. Not a lucky number.

"Gentlemen," I murmured, easing myself into the one unoccupied chair at the foot of the table. I looked around. It would not be unfair to say they were a motley crew—bald, skinny, pale, obese, acne-scarred—a bunch of adolescent misfits who had finally figured out where they belonged—the high school chess club made good in the world.

Someone cleared his throat. Another shuffled his papers. They all stared. Thirteen heads, twenty-six eyes, scrutinizing. Silence, in a room full of people who made their living from it. Well, I was as good, if not better, at this game than they were. I stared back, rotating my gaze slowly around the table, making eye contact with every single sonofabitch sitting there. I blinked, they blinked. I breathed out, they breathed in. Finally, I couldn't stand it any longer.

"What do you want from me?" I rasped.

A few unbearable moments elapsed before one of Handelman's minions spoke in a solemn but high-pitched voice.

"Why don't you tell us what's going on, Solomon."

"I don't know what you're talking about."

The body doesn't lie. I felt my left hand clenched in a

fist, nails digging into the soft flesh of my palm. My eyelids were blinking rapidly.

Silence. A roomful of analysts, waiting me out.

And then? They seemed to be saying with the tilt of their heads, their mournful expressions. *Please, go on.*

Seymour Rubens, who was seated immediately to my left, began drumming his fingers impatiently on the cherrywood table, in time with my fluttering eyelids.

"Cut it out, Grossman, you know damned well what's—"

"Hold on, Sy," said Handelman. "Solomon is entitled to have his say."

"Say *what*, Joseph?" I interrupted. "Please—tell me what's going on here."

My thespian abilities were wearing thin. My thighs had begun to shake uncontrollably. I wondered if anyone could see the twitches and spasmodic jerks of my nervous system as it began to short out.

Handelman stared me down for thirty seconds. The only sound was the ticking of the wall clock. I listened to each tick, focusing all my attention on a mole just beneath Handelman's bifocals. Finally, he stood abruptly, pushed his chair back, and strode to the bay window which overlooked Seventy-fourth Street.

"A patient of yours called my office on Thursday," he said evenly.

"Yes? Which patient?"

He stood with his profile to the room, peering out the window as if a matter of great importance was taking place on the street below.

141

"Which patient, Joseph?" I repeated, heart pounding. There was still a possibility, wasn't there? A chance that it might not all come crashing down around me?

He quickly turned and spit out the name.

"Katrina Volk."

Daughter of Hermann Muensch, exterminator extraordinaire.

"It seems," continued Handelman, "she has lodged a complaint—a very serious complaint—against you, Solomon."

"Please tell us this isn't true," said someone at the far end of the table.

"Is she delusional?"

My mind was racing. I realized they must have some fairly compelling evidence against me to have gathered in this way, without having privately and formally charged me first.

"Miss Volk insisted on coming to see me last night," said Handelman. "She was in quite a state, Solomon. It seems—"

"No, Joseph—"

I lifted my hands as if to shield myself from glare. During the month of August, while I vacationed with Ruthie and Daniel on the Cape, my secretary logged fifty-three phone calls from Katrina. *Dr. Grossman, I must speak with you at once. Dr. Grossman, please call me back. I can't sleep—I'm losing my footing—I need your help.* I did not return Katrina's calls. I was terrified of her voice, afraid it would pull me through the phone wires and into the elaborate inner workings of her psyche. Once inside her head, I would be trapped forever. Instead, I instructed my secretary to give her the name of my covering doctor. I did not even entertain the notion that I might get caught—that she might turn on me. In my panic, I suddenly lost all sense of my identity. What had happened to my perfect reserve? I came to despise myself for a weakness I had not previously known I had. And as I grew browner and more rested throughout that August, I managed to whittle my own self-hatred into a sharp blade—a blade I turned, in my mind, against Katrina. I sliced her out of my consciousness. She was a tumor. Let her grow on some other poor shmuck.

Handelman looked at me sorrowfully as he formed words too distasteful to even contemplate.

"She's claiming that you had a—sexual relationship—with her, Solomon. Is this true?"

Against my will, my shaky legs propelled me to a standing position. I had every intention of shouting *She's lying! I didn't do it!* but instead, it seemed I had lost control of my mouth as well as my legs. A soft, utterly resigned voice escaped my lips.

143

It was a sound more wailing than any that had ever come from Otto Grossman's violin. It was a complete, unabridged confession.

IT IS SAFE TO SAY that at the root of all basic neurotic wounds— at the center of most of the functioning citizens who lie on my couch —is the repetition compulsion. We do the same things over and over, and expect different results. We are prisoners of our own repressed infantile wishes.

The obvious question you might ask me is why: Why did I allow it to happen? It had a name—countertransference—and it should have been nothing more than analytic fodder. But buried

*under all the textbook knowledge and discussions ad nauseam about
transference and countertransference was something no one at the
Institute seemed willing to examine: the eventuality of human error.
We were an accident waiting to happen, Katrina and I. Planes crash.
Surgical patients die on the operating table. The only certainty is that
where there are human beings, odds on, there will one day be failure.*

*Daniel, I swear to you, though by now my words are meaning-
less: it never happened again.*

MY BREATH ELUDED ME. I gulped air thirstily like a dying
man. My hands clutched the air. My former colleagues—in an
instant they had become "former"—recoiled in horror like
doctors who see the first signs of cancer on their own bodies.
My vision began to break down. Handelman's face collapsed
into a thousand prisms, and the conference table began to
undulate, a giant wooden wave.

"You don't understand," I whispered, "it was all a huge
mistake—"

"Go on," Handelman prodded.

"It began as a game. She was trying to assuage the guilt."

"Guilt about what?"

"Her father—was a Nazi"—a pathetic, pleading note
crept into my voice—"and she knew I was a survivor. She
saw the pictures when she came to see me. She was so utterly
locked up—repressed—she had dreams of trenches, shootings,
Deutsche Christen. I made an analytic choice—foolish, I know!
—to go to the root of that repression. And to use myself—and
our transference—as a means of reaching her. It was her past,
yes? She was blocked, hurting. I thought—maybe I can help

her. And then—I don't know—she pushed too far—she made it happen—"

I trailed off, gasping, looking wildly around the room. I was looking for a nod, a blink, a glimmer of recognition, but instead I seemed to be staring into the disgusted eyes of my colleagues.

"I thought I could handle it! I should have asked for help, but I didn't know how deep all this went. My God, her father was Hermann Muensch! He was Goebbels's best friend! I had the most intense countertransference—yes, I knew that. I even tried to call you one day, Joseph—she was on her way into my office—but there was no answer. And she seduced me! Did it *to* me! It was me who was defenseless."

Rubens held a hand over his mouth in what I recognized as a trained attempt not to burst out in nervous laughter.

I abruptly stopped. Something snapped in my brain. Whatever powers of repression had allowed me to believe that it was all *her fault*—that I was somehow not to be held responsible for what happened between Katrina and myself—crumbled to nothing. I was finished. Kaput!

I began to bang my head against the wall. *Bang!* I crashed my forehead, and the first time reminded me of the *thump* of a soccer ball at the playground of the Rykestrasse, and—*bang!*—the second time I heard a delicate splintering inside my skull, a cracking I was sure no one else could hear. I continued with the steadiness of a metronome—the slow, sturdy ticking back and forth, back and forth, *bang, bang, bang,* the most comforting sound of my childhood, my father practicing arpeggios. *Quiet, Solomon, my* boychik. *Be still and listen to the music. Can you tell me: Is this a minor seventh, or a diminished fifth? Listen! Listen carefully—*

I felt hands on my back, fingers gripping my shoulders, prying me away.

"Stop him!"

"Someone *do* something!"

"Does anyone have any Valium?"

"Here!"

"No, I have it—"

Rubens left the room, then scurried back with a Dixie cup of water and wads of Kleenex. Pills were pressed first into my palm, which dangled open, refusing to curl around them. Somehow they wound up in my mouth, two pills pressed against my tongue. (If this had happened today, they would have searched for latex gloves instead of Valium.) I swallowed. I wanted out. If only someone had a syringe, liquid Valium to be injected straight into my bloodstream.

"Come, Solomon. Sit down."

I allowed Handelman to help me to a chair. I felt I was in good hands, like having a heart attack in a room full of cardiologists.

"I—couldn't—stop—"

My words were ragged, broken. The images in my mind, however, were painfully clear.

"The—worst—thing—"

"What? What's the 'worst thing,' Solomon?" Handelman gently probed.

"—Katrina—"

With her name my head fell to the table. Twenty minutes had passed, and the Valium—how many milligrams?—

had begun to take effect. Through the dizzy swirl I saw Katrina, her spine straight as she sat on my couch, very slowly unbuttoning one mother-of-pearl button at a time, giving me ample opportunity to stand up, to straighten my own spine, to deny—

But I whimpered, "no . . ."

And I wept. How many times in my life had I cried? I am not a man who cries easily, but once I begin, the floodgates open. As a boy, I was tight-lipped and dry-eyed as we closed our front door in Berlin for the last time. As an adult, I have saved my tears for happy occasions: when I received notice of my full scholarship to Yeshiva University's doctoral program, when Ruthie told me she was pregnant.

"Grossman! Snap out of it, Grossman!"

The conference room turned into a stained-glass cathedral. The light was diffused, jewel-colored. My colleagues seemed to have stepped from the flat canvases of cubist paintings, sprung to life, broken into fragments of blindingly bright ruby angles. My tear-spattered vision changed everything, transforming these men peering at me into watered-down, kind human beings who had my best interests at heart.

"We think you're in trouble. Please, Sol. We want to help!" (This from Kaplan, a slow-moving fellow with the bloodshot eyes of a St. Bernard.)

We want to help. Never before had I heard those words uttered in my direction. My parents were too busy making ends meet to worry about helping me. Early on I learned that if I was to get anywhere in life, I was going to have to forge the path myself. And what a path I forged! Swatting my way through the New York City public schools—it wasn't easy for an immigrant kid who spoke English like he had cotton balls in his mouth—talking my way into financial aid, first for college, then graduate school. I didn't know if I was smart, but I knew I was a survivor, in every sense of the word. Missing death at the hands of the Nazis had made me—how to say—ballsy, I suppose. I had a lot of chutzpah. I owed it to my relatives who hadn't been so lucky. How could I be afraid of marching into the office of the Dean of Yeshiva University? Or demanding a better grade from a professor? Or asking for Ruth Lenski's hand in marriage? Whenever I was afraid, all I had to do was conjure up Auschwitz. Then, I could work up the courage to do anything. (Little did Ruthie know that I was conjuring the death camps when I sank to one knee and proposed to her!)

"I betrayed all of you," I said tiredly. "I betrayed my own training. What must I do?"

Handelman looked above my head, as if I hadn't just spoken.

"Solomon, we need the details."

"Why? What kind of details, Joseph?"

I was prepared to do whatever was necessary. I would humble myself before them. I would abide by whatever disciplinary action they deemed appropriate, as long as they didn't try to make me resign—and as long as Ruthie didn't have to know. After all, Handelman had been like a father to me. Surely he wanted what was best for all concerned—even in the face of such a gross breach of trust.

"This could blow into something entirely out of proportion," said Handelman.

I looked at him closely. He had bags under his eyes.

Handelman had lost sleep over this. I saw his eyes flicker away from me, and pass some sort of silent communication to Rubens on his left.

"What can I do, Joseph? Tell me what you want from me."

"I'm afraid we're going to have to ask for your resignation, Solomon," Handelman said. I could see the words were painful for him.

"Oh, God, no—you can't!"

"Solomon, I don't think you understand."

"Don't do this to me! Please, I'll do anything—undergo another training analysis—"

"Miss Volk has threatened to go public with this."

"Public?"

"She's told us she'll go to the newspapers unless you resign."

In an instant, I understood. Katrina had me by the balls. In fact, she had the entire Institute by its collective balls. Later, I would think about *why*. I would mull over what I might have done differently, starting with the first time she ever darkened my office door. Deep within the caverns of my own psyche, I heard her laughing as she plastered her own yellow star on my chest. The bitch had managed to brand me for life.

I straightened myself up.

"Oh, my God," I whispered as the weight of what was happening began to sink in. As Handelman removed a prepared statement from his briefcase and pushed it across the table, I wondered if I should call an attorney. But who to call? My esteemed father-in-law Meyer Lenski? He was rumored to be connected to the Jewish mafia. I saw myself floating in the East River, a clean bullet hole in my left temple.

Auschwitz.

"I'm so sorry, Solomon, but you see the position we're in."

"Of course," I murmured as I scrawled my name across the dotted line after a drugged, cursory reading. I just wanted to get the hell out of there. I stood, feeling surprisingly solid on my legs, and looked around the table. In a single hour I had gone from favorite child to pariah. I suddenly hated them all.

"It could have happened to any one of you," I said calmly.

"Solomon, please—let us help you. Perhaps with another analysis, if we let some time go by—who knows? Reinstatement could eventually be a possibility," Handelman said.

"Sure, Joseph. I'm sure you'll all have me back."

I looked at the door, then at Joseph. I knew it would be the last time I ever stood in the Institute conference room. I walked out, leaving the door open behind me, and started down the staircase. I heard snippets of murmuring voices behind me.

"That was hellish."

"I feel terrible about this, but—

"—have to protect ourselves."

"Deal with this internally."

I pushed open the front doors of the Institute and walked slowly into the late-afternoon heat, aware of the chance that they were gathered around the bay window, watching my receding back. I even whistled a little melody, just in case they were listening. It wasn't until I reached the corner of Seventy-fourth and Columbus that I realized what I was whistling: *Deutschland, Deutschland, über alles!*

I collapsed against a mailbox on the corner, folding myself against it, wishing I could make myself small enough to fit into the slot, be sorted with the evening mail and sent wherever they send lost packages. I had nowhere to go. What could I possibly tell Ruthie? The Institute would dismiss me quietly, with no fanfare—of that I was fairly certain. But how would I explain my sudden departure to my wife?

"Young man, are you all right?"

An elderly woman wearing a perfect pillbox hat stopped in front of the mailbox with a stack of envelopes in her gloved hand.

"Yes, yes, thanks," I murmur.

"Would you mind, then?"

I moved to the side, and the slot creaked as she deposited her mail. The world went on. Old women mailed their bills, buses rumbled down Columbus Avenue, couples scurried home from their errands, grocery bags in tow.

There must be a way I could keep it all a secret. My resignation had bought me, at least, the dignity of a private defeat. The Institute wasn't the be all and end all. I'd still have my license—they weren't going to revoke that. Katrina would keep her mouth shut. No one needed to know. Perhaps we could move. Pack our bags in the middle of the night and flee—after all, I had experience in that department. In another city, we could start over. With my professional and academic credentials, we could go anywhere. London. Or San Francisco. We could sell the brownstone for a tidy sum. Make excuses to Meyer and Mama. Yes! For a moment I believed it was possible to turn bad luck into good, to unmake the bed one has made, simply by sheer force of will.

I practically trotted home.

To hell with you, Katrina Volk. You should have unbuttoned your soul instead of your blouse.

I was pumped up with adrenaline, euphoric. I would overcome. *Deutschland* was screaming through my head, my legs sprinting beneath me, and Katrina spread out on the couch before my eyes, head turned to one side, eyes strained shut. Her blouse was open, bra unhooked and dangling around her neck. Her breasts fell to each side, nipples the size of silver dollars, glistening with my saliva. Her stockings were crumpled like the molted skin of a snake on the floor. And I was on top of her, grunting like a beast, rapist that I was, driving into her so hard she grunted with each thrust, a guttural, Germanic sound that matched my own. We were at war, my patient and I, and her body was the battleground. *Deutschland, Deutschland, über alles!*

NINE

DANIEL HANGS the *Do Not Disturb* sign on the doorknob of his tenth-floor room at the airport Hyatt. Sunlight glares through the picture window, and LAX is sprawled beneath us in all its squalid splendor. They call this a view? Jets are lined up on runways like bovine creatures patiently awaiting their turn at the trough. The bed is unmade, pillow still indented with the shape of Daniel's head. The bedspread—a mauve and brown pattern designed to hide stains—has been kicked to the floor, which is carpeted in slightly deeper corresponding shades. A few cigarette butts are stubbed out in a glass ashtray, next to this morning's papers. A briefcase lies on its side, papers spilling from its open latches. What I wouldn't give for a half-hour alone in this room! I would tear through my son's suitcase, dissect his dopp kit with psychoanalytic precision: Does he use extra-strength or regular Tylenol? Lambskin or latex condoms? Waxed or unwaxed dental floss?

I would pick my way through his address book, deconstruct the contents of his wallet. Oh, to be given the chance to search for clues—to investigate the investigator.

The phone begins to ring as Daniel fiddles with the heavy, tobacco-scented drapes, trying to yank them closed. He dives across the bed and reaches it on the second ring.

"Yeah?"

He winces and holds the receiver away from his ear. Even from where I stand on the other side of the room, I can hear a man's voice shouting.

Daniel's voice, when he speaks, is low and controlled.

"Hold on a minute, let me explain—"

He listens for a moment, glancing at me quickly.

"I can't do that."

Another moment.

"Stuart, you don't understand. I simply can't get away right now."

His cheeks are two bright red spots.

"Call the local bureau. They've got perfectly competent—"

He trails off when he realizes the line has gone dead.

He places the receiver back on its hook, exhaling slowly in a long whistle.

"Shit."

"I'm sorry if I'm causing you any inconvenience," I say quietly.

"They're probably calling Washington about now."

"If you need to go—"

"One hundred and thirty-eight people are dead," he says flatly. "This is my *job*."

"I see that. I—"

"Why did you come here? Of all places, why here and now?"

"Because I knew where you were." I say simply.

"I'm thirty-one years old. For thirty-one years, you haven't known where I was?"

His cheeks grow even redder.

"Thirty."

"Pardon?"

"For the first year of your life I knew where you were."

"Oh, great."

He begins pacing the room.

"What am I going to do? I'll lose my job if I don't get down there—" He gestures out the window. "No one walks off an investigation like this. There's no excuse in the world good enough. What am I going to tell them? That my father showed up, picked this fucking moment to show his face for the first time in my life? What do you think they'll say to me? 'Gee, Danny-boy, how touching. Go have your reunion with Daddy. We'll hold down the fucking fort.'"

His face twists into a sneer as he mimics bitterly.

"Why don't you go? I'll wait here," I say calmly, my heart leaping at the possibility.

"You think I'm going to leave you alone?" he practically spits at me. "You think I believe, for a single solitary second, that if I go you'll still be here when I get back?"

"I give you my word—"

He sits heavily on the bed, shooting me a look that stops me cold. It tells me that my promises are like pebbles in his mouth. He can spit them back at me, and they will hurt.

"It's not like there aren't a dozen guys out there who can do the same job," he says.

"What, exactly, do you do?" I ask.

My question dangles weakly in the air, the echo of my own voice the worst form of torture. He pushes himself off the bed with a sigh, walks to the closet, and slides it open to reveal a mini-refrigerator. He pulls out a Perrier.

"Want anything?"

He's not going to answer my question.

"Vodka," I say casually, "if you have it."

"Is that a good idea?" he asks.

"I'm fine now."

"Catch!" he says, tossing a tiny bottle of Smirnoff to me. It sails through the air, my medicine—all my life I have treated alcoholics and drug addicts, but I have never understood from the inside what a mouthwatering craving it is—the thirst for release from self-loathing.

I twist open the top and take a gulp before I realize Daniel is standing in front of me, offering a glass. A small, bemused smile plays at his lips.

"I guess it really does run in families," he says.

"What?"

"Never mind."

He takes a sip of his Perrier.

"Don't you want a *real* drink?" I ask him, desperate for company.

"Never touch the stuff," he says.

He watches as I down the small bottle in three long gulps. *Salut! Na zdarovya! Prosit! Cheers!* I can't help myself.

Can I ask him for another? And another? All the mini-refrig-erators in this Hyatt would not be enough.

"You're in real trouble, old man—aren't you?" he asks softly.

"Trouble? Don't be silly."

The room is revolving.

"How long has this been going on?"

"What?"

He pauses, bites his thumbnail.

"Go ahead—say what's on your mind—"

"You're a full-fledged drunk."

I act as if Daniel is a patient confronting me. (The patient, unlike the customer, is always wrong.)

"And what makes you say that?"

"Look at you!"

He pulls me over to the bureau, turns my face so that once again, I am staring into a mirror. I don't mind, really, as long as my son's hands are on my cheeks.

My ghost-self stares back at me. During all the years I shaved in the shower to avoid my own reflection in the bath-room mirror, my face has wrinkled into a map of life's trou-bles. My eyes are hooded, glowing like dying embers.

"I don't usually do this," I say. "In fact, I hardly drink at all. I'm just so nervous."

"I understand," says Daniel, struggling to believe me. I look at his reflection and am pierced with a moment of sanity, a hot searing pain through the center of my heart.

"I am not a drunk. I am a psychoanalyst," I say, as if one precludes the other.

Daniel buries his head in his hands and peers up at me through a web of fingers.

"A shrink?" he practically chokes. "A *shrink?*"

"I am a senior supervising analyst at one of the finest institutes in New York," I say primly, "and have been in private practice for over thirty-five years."

I leave off the defining low points of my career, neglecting to mention the dismissal from the Institute, the newspaper clippings. It slowly dawns on me that not knowing my son for thirty years actually has a small but exciting upside: there is nothing stopping me from reinventing myself. Clearly he knows nothing of my past. Ruthie made the wise decision to tell him I was dead. She knew, no matter how horrible a portrait she might have painted of me, Daniel would have gone searching if he had the slightest inkling that I was alive.

The phone begins to ring again.

Daniel looks at it, then at me, calculating.

"If I go down there for a half-hour, will you just—wait here?"

"Aren't you going to answer the phone?"

"I know what they want," he says tersely. "I really have to go. Swear to me you'll be here when I get back?"

"I swear."

"Sorry—it's just—I have to talk to some people."

"It's all right."

Is it ever.

"A half-hour. Then we'll have some lunch."

I glance at my watch. I have no idea what day it is, what time it is. Three o'clock.

He grabs his hotel key and rushes out the door.

Jackpot!

I count slowly to twenty, waiting until I'm certain Daniel has descended in the elevator. He left so quickly he forgot his wallet, which he had tossed on the bureau when we first walked in the room. Forgot, indeed! Every Freudian knows there are no incidental lapses of memory, no simple slips-of-tongue. Clearly, my son *wants* me to go through his wallet. I heave myself out of my chair and prepare to do his unconscious bidding.

The leather is soft and worn at the edges, embossed on the inside with the gold Mark Cross logo. An expensive wallet—perhaps a gift from his mother. How would poor Ruthie have felt if she had known that I would one day break free of my own shackles and track down our son? That she would be dead and buried on some Connecticut hillside and I would be here, in an airport Hyatt, riffling through the contents of Daniel's wallet? There is a reason for the expression "turning over in her grave."

Daniel Gross
2165 Kalorama Road N.W. Apt. #207
Washington, DC 20009

His face, several years younger, peers up at me from behind a cloudy plastic window. The address on his driver's license is as exotic to me as if it were in Tanzania. I close my eyes and try to envision his apartment: a cluttered second-floor walk-up in an elegant townhouse, floors covered with the Lenskis' orientals. Is he a reader? Does he listen to music?

I try to fill in the details of the picture, but come up blank. I don't have enough information.

I pry my fingers into a bulging side flap and pull out an impressive assortment of credit cards: American Express, Visa, MasterCard, Optima, Discover, Exxon, Getty, Saks, and Nordstrom. He uses MCI, flies Delta, and is a charter member of the recently opened Holocaust Museum in Washington—a not-insignificant piece of trivia I file away for further thought.

In the billfold there are four twenty-dollar bills; a receipt from a Washington florist for an arrangement to be sent to someone named McCall only a few blocks from where I live in New York; a slip of paper from a fortune cookie which reads *there is an exciting stranger in your future.* Like hell, there is.

I spread it all out on the bureau like pieces to a puzzle. What does it mean? If I were a detective, what would I make of these clues? Clearly he is a man of means; the credit cards and seventy-five dollar florist's bill attest to that. But I already knew that my son would be financially stable, if not filthy rich. After all, he is the only grandchild of Meyer Lenski. Jews believe in passing their money through the generations, never touching a dime. No doubt, Meyer and Mama left Daniel quite a tidy little fortune—probably with attached strings to last his whole lifetime.

I feel through the wallet, bending it slightly to make sure it's entirely empty, and come across a small slit in the leather where two stamp-sized photographs have been carefully tucked away. I pull them out gingerly. Even before I look at them, something tells me I have stumbled across something more revealing than any credit card or fortune cookie. In the first black-and-white photo, Daniel has his arms wrapped around a lovely, long-haired blonde. Both of them are laughing, heads bent together, her hair falling around them like a tent. The second picture nearly stops my heart: a little girl, no more than two or three, stares at the camera. Her hair is the color of wheat, but her eyes are dark brown. Dark brown pools into which I find myself falling, flailing, drowning.

I go over to the mini-fridge and grab myself another vodka. There is no doubt in my mind, none whatsoever, that I am looking into the eyes of my son's daughter.

SHE IS SO BEAUTIFUL, Danny! Who would have thought such an angel could be born of Grossman genes! In her face I see a whole family history unfold like the pages of a book I thought had been burned to ashes: my father's brother, your uncle Manny (may he rest in peace), in the curve of her jaw, my aunt Reba's apple cheeks flushed beneath those unmistakable dark brown eyes.

The hair she must get from her mother.

When were you going to tell me? That the rusty Grossman chain has not been broken, that it continues in the bright, shining eyes of a little girl?

I turn over the photograph. In a faint, almost illegible penciled script, I make out: Jenna at 30 months.

Another reason to live.

I HEAR DANIEL'S KEY in the door just as I am reassembling the contents of his wallet. He fumbles with those ridiculous card keys they use these days, buying me an extra few seconds to stuff the bills back in the billfold, the credit cards into their proper place, but the photos—I don't have time. I quickly slip them into my shirt pocket just as the latch clicks open.

"Hey!" He raises his eyebrows, surprised to see me standing.

"Hi, I was just—" I cough as the breath mint I popped in my mouth catches in my throat.

He looks around the room, his gaze sliding over his wallet on the bureau, which I have left on its side, just as I found it. I never even had a chance to sneak a look at his luggage. This half-hour has whizzed by faster than any half-hour in recent memory.

"What have you been doing?" he asks.

"Oh, nothing much," I say. "Just sitting here dreaming."

Dreaming of my granddaughter.

I feel for the second vodka bottle with the toe of my shoe, then gently nudge it under the dresser. If he opens the refrigerator, he'll find it missing. My legs are wobbly, and my breath smells of spearmint Certs.

"I've decided we should change hotels," he says.

"Why's that? It's perfectly comfortable here—"

"*I'm* not comfortable. I'd rather not be around half the people I work with." he answers shortly.

"You mean—did you—?"

"I've removed myself from the investigation."

"I see."

He starts walking quickly around the room, throwing his few belongings into the top of his duffel bag. Clearly he is a man used to packing and unpacking.

I squint out the window at the concrete sprawl of LAX

ten floors beneath us. From here I can't see anything, but I know the wreck is there. The people I met last night on the World Air van are now milling around the morgue, most likely wading through miles of dental records and red tape.

"I'm sorry," I say gruffly.

"Let's not talk about it. I called the Bel Air and reserved a suite."

"The Bel Air?" I croak.

"Is there a problem?"

"Isn't that very expensive?"

He stops packing for a moment and looks up at me.

"Money is one of the only problems I *don't* have."

I decide not to tell him that, out of every luxury hotel in Los Angeles, he has chosen the one where his mother and I spent the second night of our honeymoon before flying to Hawaii.

Daniel slings our bags over his shoulder as we ride down the elevator together wordlessly, then walk through the crowded lobby, past signs pointing to more NTSB press briefings. He stares ahead as if he has blinders on, holding my elbow, steering me through the throng.

"Look," I say hoarsely, "I know I've really screwed up your situation here."

His lips are one straight line.

"I wasn't thinking—about whether I was intruding—"

I am suddenly, miserably aware of the grief all around us. An older couple sits on a couch in the center of the lobby, holding hands, their faces drawn and gray. An Indian man in a turban huddles over a pay phone, speaking rapidly into the receiver, eyes closed.

"It doesn't matter. As I said, I'm off the job," Daniel says evenly.

"Are you going to get into trouble over this?"

"Probably not. Let's drop it."

In the flatness behind his eyes I see my own defenses, and understand that Daniel is cutting himself off from this investigation the same way I disengage from a troubled patient who terminates analysis prematurely. When forced to walk away from a wreck, it's best not to turn around and stare.

The valet pulls up with the car, and we climb inside.

"Top up or down?" Daniel asks.

"Down."

I want to feel the wind against my face, breathe in the soft California air. A week ago, I could not even have dreamt this—my son and I in a convertible cruising the freeways of Los Angeles! I roll up my shirt sleeves. The photographs in my breast pocket are warm against my chest. They have given me a peculiar, sneaky strength.

Century Boulevard to the San Diego Freeway to Sunset Boulevard, Daniel drives like Evil Knievel. He seems to know his way around this town like a citizen. It makes me jealous. When has he been to Los Angeles before—and with whom? A thousand questions perch on my tongue, threatening to tumble off at any second. I notice a very slight variation in color on the ring finger of his left hand as he tightly grips the steering wheel. A small muscle bunches in his jaw as he weaves from lane to lane, eyes squinting behind sunglasses. He drives not carelessly, but with great determination. Is he married to Jenna's mother? Or divorced? How do you ask your grown son a question which is already a matter of public record? The census bureau knows more about him than I do.

I clear my throat and begin with a harmless question.

"How do you know your way around so well?"

My voice gets lost in the hot wind blowing off Sunset Boulevard as we whiz past suburban houses and the absurdly grand mansions of Beverly Hills built nearly as close to one another as the rowhouses in Queens. As we drive with the top down, I am convinced my hairline is receding. The sun beats down on my already-pink scalp. I feel like an advertisement for a car commercial—that is, as long as I don't look in the mirror.

"You certainly know your way around," I try again loudly as we pass the green expanse of the UCLA campus.

He smiles, his hands easing up on the steering wheel as he turns onto Bellagio Road and begins winding uphill through the lush greenery of Bel Air. We are flanked on both sides by gates, bougainvillea, intercoms. A Porsche pokes its snubby nose around a blind curve. We cruise past peach-colored houses, rose vines climbing their thick walls, dripping off rooftops like icing on wedding cakes.

"I've spent a lot of time in this town," he says.

Town? Los Angeles has no locus. Like a cluster of tumors whose origin is suspect, this is a city without edges, suppressed only by the shores of the Pacific Ocean.

"Doing what?"

"I—"

He stops, runs his fingers through his hair. He has two deep creases in his forehead.

"Let's talk about it later," he says quite politely.

Why the mystery? I eye him suspiciously. He is blinking rapidly, as if fending off a painful image. Perhaps I should hire a detective. I have no intention of telling him the unabridged story of my life—but I plan to know every last detail of his. Of course, I know this should be a two-way street. But I believe if I tell Daniel the unedited version of my life, he will screech to the curb, open the door, and unceremoniously dump me on the nearest lawn. After all, who wants a failure as a father? Why would he waste his time? No, I will fight my way through the maze my mind has become and, with the help of my dear friend Smirnoff, invent myself from the ground up. I will paint a Renaissance portrait worthy of hanging in the Louvre: A kindly psychoanalyst, descended from Freud himself, who lost his family in the war but persevered—his moral imperatives his only compass in a world rife with evil institutes and sinister father-in-laws.

Bel Air has hardly changed in the thirty-five years since my honeymoon; only the electric gates and posted signs of alarm systems dotting the ivy-covered walls are testament to the late twentieth century. Labyrinthine roads twist uphill, leading to larger, even more secluded estates. I breathe in deeply, filling my lungs with the scent of freshly mowed grass.

"Beautiful, isn't it?" Daniel shouts over the wind.

I nod. A mother and her teenaged daughter, both wearing tennis whites and sneakers, amble down a long driveway, racquets slung over their shoulders. The weight of what I have lost in my life rests on my chest heavily. It is difficult to breathe. I pat my shirt pocket, tracing the photographs beneath my fingers.

Small signs are everywhere: *Private, Guard Dog, No Trespassing*. We are driving further into a neighborhood of mansions, a sweetly scented ghetto of the super-rich, a country whose language I don't speak. Daniel seems perfectly at ease, the wind blowing his hair back from his face. I study him. He is my son—no doubt about that. Still, the Lenski genes have imprinted themselves on his profile. I can see Meyer's strong chin, the slope of Ruthie's high forehead. But above all, I sense the Lenski entitlement as surely as if it were a genetic trait—a second-generation Jewish noblesse oblige flowing through his veins. Daniel is perfectly at ease driving this convertible through the hills of Bel Air. There is no question he was raised in the lap of luxury. He has never vomited his way across the Atlantic or packed his essential belongings into a single suitcase.

We pull into the driveway of the Bel Air Hotel. A vein throbs along the left side of my throat. I place two fingers on it and feel the blood pounding too fast as we come to a stop at the canopied entrance. A valet in a tan-and-white uniform leaps to our service.

"Checking in?"

"Yes, please." Daniel hops nimbly out of the driver's seat and hands the car keys to the valet.

A small bridge arcs over a pond where three swans float serenely, their long necks curved into their bodies as they sleep. For a single, sentimental moment, I think that Ruthie and I once fed bread crumbs to these swans' parents or perhaps their grandparents—but then I stop myself from such romantic drivel. The swans we fed on our honeymoon are as related to these as the Lenskis are related to the Grossmans.

These swans are from a pet store. We are in the land of illusion, where nothing is as it seems.

We walk through the main entrance, past framed and signed photos of Princess Grace, Jack Kennedy, Aristotle Onassis. History doesn't change, it only accumulates. I wonder if Jenna Gross will walk through the halls of this luxurious hotel some day, retracing the footsteps of her grandfather and father without even knowing it, trudging the same worn path as her ghosts. Could this be the definition of upward mobility as we claw our way through the generations—from Berlin to Bel Air?

A bellboy leads us to our room. We follow him through pink sandstone arches, past a small stone gargoyle spitting water from his mouth. Potted palms, gardens of pink and white begonias. I feel myself floating on some current of hidden memory, down the same paths Ruthie and I walked, arm-in-arm, over three decades ago. Some split firewood is stacked in an iron basket to the side of Suite 114, which is perfectly situated between terrace and pool. Nights get cool here, even as the days burn through a thick blanket of smog. A room service tray has been left outside the door next to ours. As the bellboy opens the door, I bend down to examine the contents. A small tin of beluga caviar scraped clean, a single, paper-thin slice of smoked salmon stuck to the edge of a china plate, an empty bottle of Veuve Clicquot, a wilted white rose in a bud vase. Not bad for the middle of the afternoon. I can imagine what's happening on the other side of the Do Not Disturb sign.

Daniel precedes me into our suite. Thirty years do make a difference. The Bel Air has done quite a job redecorating its rooms. I guess this shouldn't surprise me. Light, airy linen, peach-colored duvet covers, cabbage-rose wallpaper have replaced the heavier furnishings of three decades ago. Even the master bedroom, which now has a peach silk upholstered headboard, does not remind me of the three nights I spent here with Ruthie. What did I expect? Did I think I'd see her ghost—a lovely, dark-haired creature spread across the quilt, arms flung wide? Or sitting in a wing chair next to a blazing fireplace, perhaps, nibbling on a room service roll? The corners of my eyes sting. Ruthie is nowhere to be found—and Daniel, who was not, as they say, even a glimmer in my eye in those days, is standing by the living room window, looking over our private patio, his blue eyes guarded and numb.

He turns to me.

"Is this all right?" he asks, making a sweeping gesture around the room.

"Daniel, it's beautiful. Excessive, but beautiful."

"Are you hungry?"

"You bet."

"Do you want room service, or should we go to the restaurant?"

"Let's go to the restaurant," I say, sensing that the intimacy of these closed quarters, spacious as they are, is too much for us.

WE SIT OUTSIDE on a flagstone patio overlooking the pond. The maître d' tells Daniel they've stopped serving lunch, but a twenty-dollar bill—one of the very same bills I fingered just an hour ago—seems to turn back the clock.

A hot wind rustles the menus in our hands as we sneak glances at each other, awkward as two people on a first date. The waiter hovers until Daniel impatiently places both our orders.

"Two tuna burgers, medium-rare. Diet Coke for me— and—?"

"Club soda," I say casually.

"—and a club soda for my—father."

We stare at each other, the word *father* hanging in the air as a busboy pulls our fan-shaped napkins out of the water glasses, then fills them.

"I wish they'd just leave us alone," he mutters.

I nod, suddenly tongue-tied. My face is flushed, and my armpits are damp under my jacket. I watch as Daniel continues to study his menu. Of course he's finding this hard— perhaps even harder than I am. After all, I've had thirty years to prepare for this moment. He's had no time at all.

"So tell me." I clear my throat. "Why did you decide to do what you do? It must be very painful work."

He smiles weakly.

"Is that really what you want to talk about?"

"It's as good a place to start as any."

He shrugs.

"Well, I suppose—in a way—it's not that different from what *you* do. I investigate plane crashes. A disaster happens, and I try to trace it back to what went wrong."

I look at him, bemused.

"What?"

"It just seems a surprising choice. I would have expected you would be—"

"A doctor? A lawyer like Meyer?" he snaps.

"Something like that."

"Sorry to disappoint you—but I had my problems, particularly when I was younger."

"You don't disappoint me, Daniel," I say quietly.

He drops his head, fiddles with the tassle along the spine of the menu. A bee buzzes around his ear, settling for an instant on his cheek. He doesn't seem to notice.

"Now I suppose you're wondering whether I've ever been in therapy. Isn't that what all shrinks want to know?"

"The thought did cross my mind," I say wryly.

He is silent.

"Well, *have* you ever been in therapy?" I finally ask, my voice slipping into a familiar cadence when I pose a question I have asked a thousand patients, maybe more.

He hesitates a moment. Is this going to be another one of those *verboten* subjects? I can see him weighing his answer.

"Yes," he says slowly, and leaves it at that.

I can't help myself.

"May I ask when? And with whom? Are you still going?" The questions fire across the table rapidly, *rat-tat-tat.*

"Slow down," he laughs. "Let's see. I started when I was in college—"

"Which was where?"

"Yale—"

Meyer's alma mater.

"—and I saw someone in New Haven for a couple of years—"

"What was his name?"

"*Her* name was Dr. Barbara Krasnoff—"

"Don't know her."

"Does it matter?"

I realize I'm relieved not to have known Daniel's analyst. Not to have to live with the knowledge that someone in my professional circle actually knew my son all these years.

"Go on."

"Then I started up again when I was in graduate school—"

"Which was where?"

Questions swim inside me, colliding with each other, merging, blending, spilling into one another like spermatazoa beneath a microscope—lost, blind, but with a great sense of urgency.

"I went to UCLA for a year, but then I dropped out."

So that's why he knows Los Angeles so well.

"I see."

"I got married."

"What is her name?" I prod.

"McCall."

Ah, yes. The flowers.

"What kind of name is that?"

"You mean, is she Jewish?"

The thought had not quite formulated itself.

"Well yes, now that you mention it—"

"No."

So my son married a shiksa. Why should this surprise me? If you were to sketch a psychological outline of our family tree, the branches withered and misshapen from lack of care—you would see, just beneath the surface, that striving, futile longing to be a part of something different, something better—and that striving grows exponentially with each new generation. The stakes get higher. So I married the daughter of Meyer Lenski, and my son married someone with a name that sounds like it was on the Declaration of Independence.

"You've been divorced for—?"

"Two years."

"Where does she live?"

"New York. The Upper West Side," he says, his voice flat, mouth barely moving. I watch his lips as if the words might suck themselves back in. I can't imagine it. My son's ex-wife lives in my neighborhood.

"Here—" he says, digging into his pants pocket. "I have a picture—"

"Daniel, no!"

He pauses and looks at me, startled.

"What's the matter?"

"I—"

Our drinks and the tuna burgers arrive all at once. I take a quick sip of my club soda as soon as the waiter puts it down, and feel a stabbing pain in my head. The pain is fiery; my scalp burns. I close my eyes against a vision of my corpse, disfigured beyond recognition, charred black like the victims of the wreck. My breath is coming in short gasps despite my efforts to control it.

Daniel's face is frozen, his hand still hovering over his pocket. I twist my mouth into a smile as I take the napkin from my lap and pat the beads of sweat on my forehead.

"Are you all right?"

"I think so—"

"What is it?"

"I—"

White-hot fingers reach inside my head and squeeze once, twice.

"Maybe I should see a doctor," I moan, frightened.

"No shit."

I close my eyes and try to steady my breath. The pain subsides as quickly as it arrived. I lean forward, elbows on the table.

"I'm all right. Probably just one of those flash migraines," I reassure him.

He looks shaken, even whiter than usual.

"Please—take care of yourself."

His voice breaks. Beneath all the hard-bitten detective bravado, he's only thirty-one years old. When I was his age, I was still a child in many ways, though I thought I was a big shot.

"I'm not going anywhere," I promise him.

His losses are written across his face. They rest in the pale blue shadows beneath his eyes.

"So tell me," I prod gently. Anything to stop him from reaching for his wallet. "You were talking about your marriage to—McCall. Why so young?"

"I—I don't know. We were divorced after two years," he says.

"Here"—he rummages through his wallet—"I was going to show you a picture—"

Shit.

"Daniel—"

A good poker player knows the right time to fold. I reach into my own shirt pocket and produce the two photographs of McCall and their daughter, sliding them across the table face down, until I am touching Daniel's fingers. I place my hand over his, on top of the photographs.

"I'm a bit of an investigator myself."

ONCE I SAW YOU and your mother walking west on Fifty-seventh Street. It was the week before Christmas, and the entire boulevard was twinkling in the holiday dusk, awash in light. You were carrying Ruthie's shopping bags—a rainbow assortment of lavender, brown-and-white stripes, shiny silver with handles tied with multicolored ribbons.

Ruthie was wearing a full-length mink, and she looked—how to say it?—well tended. I glanced at her left hand to check for a wedding ring, but she was wearing dark leather gloves. You were almost grown by then—I figured you must be sixteen—and you were holding your mother's elbow protectively, steering her through the throng as you carried all her packages. You already towered over her, though there was something delicate about you, some indefinable grace which is sometimes forged from loss.

She saw me, Daniel. I was walking east—on my way to Bloomingdale's, where I planned to buy one of the only gifts on my Christmas list, for my secretary, Mrs. Dodd. Ruthie and I locked eyes for a single instant, and without missing a beat, she directed you across the street where a Salvation Army choir was singing "Silent Night."

I followed. I stood no more than five feet away. Ruthie pulled you even closer, stared straight ahead. The only sign that she was afraid was a slight tensing in her jaw. I knew she was clenching her teeth, mind racing. There was no Big Daddy around to protect her.

You looked confused—why was your mother listening to off-key Christmas carols?—but you waited patiently by her side. Such a good boy. My fingers tingled as I watched you with equal parts longing and terror. I wondered what would happen if I just walked right up to you and introduced myself. I rapidly came to the conclusion that Ruthie would start screaming for the cops.

Voices wailed around us. "All is calm, all is bright . . ." as Ruthie spun around and stared straight at me. You followed her gaze to see what she was looking at—why was your mother giving the evil eye to some skinny guy in an old overcoat?—and under the heat of your gazes I felt myself disappearing into the busy crowd of lost souls.

Do you remember that winter dusk, Daniel? Think back fifteen years to a cold night on Fifty-seventh Street. Does a dark-haired man in an overcoat come to mind—a man with eyes tearing from the icy wind? Hear the music. "Sleep in heavenly peace . . ."

TEN

I SPRINTED UP THE BROWNSTONE steps and quickly un-
locked the front door, rehearsing my magnificent lies. They
shone and glanced off the gleaming parquet floor like prisms
of light. *The surprise party for Bernheim is in the planning stages, I*
would tell Ruthie, but, darling, there's something more serious I
need to discuss with you. I have quite suddenly received an offer to
become Chairman of the Department of Clinical Psychology at the
University of Paris. Yes, yes, chérie, I know I don't speak French.
But, mon dieu, I will learn!

I marched down the hall.

"Ruthie?"

No answer.

"Ruthie, are you back yet?"

A splinter of light poked from beneath the closed door
to the den, a room we almost never used. The knob glistened.
I turned it, and the door swung open without a sound. The

back of my father-in-law's bald head rested against our couch, a cracked green leather affair. Shiny black shoes tapped against the coffee table. Mama Lenski was sitting next to him, her eyes red-rimmed, swollen. Her hair was a mess—a beehive gone awry—and her fingers, grasping a crumpled white hankie—were devoid of her usual diamond bands. Mama's hands without rings—this is what I noticed. Something was very wrong. I scanned the room like a burglar, looking for traps and all visible means of escape. It took a moment before I saw Ruthie, all curled up in a window seat, clutching a pillow to her stomach, rocking back and forth.

"Who died?"

I hadn't even meant to speak the words. As soon as he heard my voice, Meyer leapt to his feet. His face was beet red and a throbbing vein popped from his forehead, splitting his face unevenly in two. In his fist he brandished a piece of paper rolled around itself like a scepter.

"You." He actually bared his teeth at me. I had always assumed the rumors about my father-in-law's temper to be greatly exaggerated, but as I looked into his bulging eyes, I wondered.

"Oh, Solomon," Mama moaned. "How could you?"

Ruthie rocked herself like a catatonic, staring out the window. The sun was sinking behind Riverside Park, casting a fiery amber glaze across the front of our brownstone.

"Ruthie?" I moved toward her warily, ignoring Meyer and Mama. After all, she was my *wife*. "What's wrong, baby?"

Slowly, she turned her head in my direction. Her eyes were round, darker than I'd ever seen them, pupils huge with shock. I reached out and brushed a tendril from her wet cheek. I touched her shoulder lightly. She was quivering. I heard an echo of Mama's voice—*Solomon, how could you*—it could mean only one thing. But I couldn't imagine—it seemed impossible—

"Ruthie, please. Talk to me."

"Solomon"—she drew out my name in one long breath —"in a million years I never thought you were capable of a thing like this."

"What? How—?" I looked around wildly, suddenly feeling the need for protection. On the mantel above the fireplace was an antique bronze sword we had found on a trip to the Catskills. I wanted to grab the sword, unsheath it, and take on the entire Lenski clan—*en garde*; better yet, I could impale myself. How was it possible? I was past trying to deny what Ruthie obviously already knew. Too much had happened in one day. I couldn't make sense of it. My brain stopped functioning—all I could hear inside my head was one long scream.

I stood still. Ruthie was shaking, and I wanted to take off my jacket and drape it around her shoulders, but I didn't dare. I had relinquished all rights to my wife. Her body was now off-limits. And then I understood: Ruthie would be leaving me—with Daniel—and Meyer and Mama were her sentries. They would pack her up, escort her down the brownstone steps and into a waiting cab. They would create a wall around their daughter and grandchild. It would take me thirty years to climb over it.

"Sonofabitch!"

Meyer crossed the room in two strides and thwacked me in the chest with the rolled-up document. He stood uncomfortably close to me as I unfurled the piece of paper and saw that it was a carbon of a typewritten, single-spaced paragraph of a story that was to appear in the following day's *New York Post*.

"Tell us it isn't true, Solly," moaned Mama Lenski. "Tell us you didn't do this."

"What," Meyer shouted at Mama, "you think the *New York Post* is making it up? And not just the *Post*, but the *Daily News*, too? Just wait—by tomorrow it'll be in the *Times*, the *Journal*—"

I opened my mouth and closed it again, a hooked fish gasping for air. Meyer shoved the piece of paper into my chest again, this time nearly putting his finger through it.

"Read it," he sneered. "Did you think about *this* when your pecker was leading you around on a leash?"

"Meyer!" Mama gasped, and pointed to Ruthie, rocking there. "Think!"

Tears streamed down Ruthie's face so hard I thought they would leave permanent tracks. Was she listening? She seemed cut off from the rest of us. She fingered the fringe of a pale gold pillow, smoothing the fine strands as if they were a child's silken hair. Her lips were swollen. Ruthie was not brought up to deal with even the ordinary anguish of life— but this, this shame, was more than she should have to tolerate. She didn't deserve this. My heart lurched toward her, followed by my feet.

"Ruthie—"

"Don't you dare go near her!" Meyer bellowed. He stood between me and my wife. "You touch her with your filthy hands and you're dead. Understand?"

The whites of his eyes were rheumy, like slightly runny yolks. In certain circles, *you're dead* is more than a figure of speech.

I glanced at the carbon. Meyer Lenski was part of New York's innermost circle, at the center of a smug band of men who wore pinstriped suits to lunch at the Harmonic Club, made things tick, protected their own. No doubt, a little birdie at the newspaper had hand-delivered this unsavory news to Meyer. He wasn't powerful enough to *stop* the news —but he paid handsomely to receive notice of it before the rest of us.

A 34-year-old psychologist, Solomon H. Grossman, Ph.D., has been accused by an unidentified female patient of sexual molestation, according to Joseph Handelman, Ph.D., Director of the Institute for Psychoanalysis. Dr. Grossman, who practices psychoanalysis in Manhattan, and is the son-in-law of Meyer Lenski, the former Manhattan district attorney, has resigned from his post as Supervising Analyst, pending investigation.

Elsewhere in the house, Daniel began to cry. His thin wail pierced the silence in the den, then was quickly hushed. I imagined his nanny holding him, his rosebud lips slurping at his bottle.

Ruthie stood up. She swayed slightly on her feet, disoriented.

"I'd better tend to Daniel," she said quietly, then moved around her father, keeping him between us at all times. Mama followed Ruthie out of the den. Their heels clicked upstairs.

My in-laws had taken over. I heard Mama overhead, walking down the hall to Daniel's nursery. A door opened and closed. The nanny shuffled away. I was deeply familiar with the daily rhythms of my own home—rhythms which were being systematically taken apart as Meyer and I waited downstairs. I heard the thud of a heavy suitcase being dragged from the hall closet. The screech of hangers being lifted from closet rods. Cosmetics jars clinking. None of it surprised me. In my deepest secret self, I had always known that my life would come to this. Destruction begets destruction. Ruin is atavistic. For a brief window in time, I had imagined that I might break my family chain, climb on the tower of Grossman bones and build a monumental life—a life worthy of having survived the ruin that preceded it. But no. In a single moment, I had taken everything that mattered to me—my family, my reputation— and snapped it like a brittle branch.

I shuffled past Meyer—there was no reason left to be afraid—and sank into the leather couch. He walked to the fireplace, pulled a cigar from his blazer pocket, bit off the end, and threw it on the hearth. He had the barrel-chested build of a street fighter—a grown hoodlum in a french-cuffed, monogrammed shirt.

He clamped the cigar with his teeth, lit a match, then rolled it around until the whole fat end was glowing orange.

"Meyer, I—"

He waved me away airily, like I was a problem he had already solved.

"Solomon. Listen very closely."

He sucked on the cigar, shaking his head slowly, as if he was sorry for what he was about to say. Meyer had always liked me, in spite of himself. I think he admired my guts. He hadn't been ecstatic when I asked him for Ruthie's hand in marriage—I think he had in mind a Bronfman instead of a Grossman—but he had nonetheless given us his blessing.

"Do you remember what I told you, before you married my daughter?"

"Yes," I answered quietly.

"What did I say?"

I stared at my thumbnail.

"*What did I say?*" he suddenly bellowed.

"You told me—to be good to her—" I whispered.

"*And is this what you call being good to her?*" he screamed. He turned his back to me and gazed out the window.

"The ride is over, Solomon."

"Sorry?"

"The ride. Is over."

Staccato. Like the sound of gunfire. Like the sound of Ruthie's heels skittering across the floor upstairs. Rat-tat-tat.

"You are out of my daughter's life," he said evenly. His face returned to its usual sallow color, blood pressure dropping to normal.

"Now wait a minute, Meyer—I think that's up to Ruthie—"

Mama Lenski appeared at the door. She had smoothed her hair and applied a fresh coat of red lipstick. She carried a bundle in her arms, swaddled in a pale blue blanket. I saw the top of Daniel's head, a downy patch of pink skin. In the dim hallway, Ruthie was standing in a dark cotton dress, holding a suitcase in each hand.

"I'll carry him, Mama—"

She dropped her suitcases and gathered Daniel to her chest, held him tight as she carefully avoided my gaze.

I sprang from the couch. My chest was constricted, and I was short of breath. It was happening too fast.

"Ruthie—honey—hold on, you can't—"

"Just watch me, Solomon."

"I didn't mean—that's not what I meant! Please—give me a minute. Let me talk to you alone, without—"

I waved my hand at Meyer and Mama. I was panting. For a moment I saw Ruthie waver.

"Did you do it?" she asked.

I stared at her.

"Just answer the question, Solomon."

If only I had been a good liar!

"Did you? Yes or no?"

"It's more complicated than that—" I choked out.

An evil little smile crossed her face like a single cloud in an otherwise clear sky.

"No, it isn't complicated at all," she said softly. "Look how easy it is."

With that, she hurled her house keys at me. I ducked, and they sailed through the den, a bright shining metal ball, keys to a fallen kingdom.

"Let's go," Meyer said gruffly. He grabbed the suitcases, and he and Mama preceded Ruthie out of the brownstone into a waiting Checker cab.

"Ruthie, wait!" I followed her down the hall.

She stood at the open front door for a moment, she and Daniel framed by the blue-gray dusk, a sliver of the setting sun casting an eerie orange glow across the sidewalk. The way she was holding him, she almost looked pregnant again, her baby bundled deep inside where no one—not even I—could touch him.

"Let me just see Daniel—" I pleaded with her.

"Not now. We'll talk."

"Just for a minute—"

I grabbed at the blue blanket, but she was already in motion, pulling Daniel away from me. And I was left holding the warm, soft remnant of a life. Through the taxi's back window, I saw all three adult Lenski heads bobbing like bright shiny apples. I prayed Ruthie was cradling Daniel's head to her chest, shielding him in case of sudden stops. I closed my eyes against a vision of Daniel's face slamming against the glass partition. The fantasies had begun—images which would plague me for years—of harm coming to my child. I stood on the stoop, holding the blanket to my nose, long after the cab rounded the corner.

IT WAS A SATURDAY NIGHT. I tried to remember if Ruthie and I had plans—I had a dim recollection of a dinner party. It all seemed so far away. I slumped to the floor just inside the front door, and did not move until the sun had set on the other side of the Hudson, and the hall was pitch black. When I finally got to my feet, I went into the kitchen and scavenged beneath the sink for a bottle of scotch. I didn't bother with a glass—just took the bottle with me to my office. It was the only place I felt safe that night—the first of the many thousands of nights I have since spent alone. My files, papers, books anchored me. The language of psychoanalysis—a rhetoric born out of the human condition of suffering—was comforting in its sheer volume. I scanned the shelves of my library. The books were all in order, arranged alphabetically by subject, *narcissism* nestled against *necrophilia*, and so forth. My pillows were plumped, and the long fringe of the oriental was combed out perfectly. The maid had been in that morning, and a slight hint of walnut oil lingered in the air. I looked again at the crumpled sheet of paper Meyer had left behind, which I had folded into my pants pocket. . . . *accused by an unidentified female patient of sexual molestation, according to Joseph Handelman, Ph.D., Director of the Institute . . .*

Handelman, that fuck! What was in it for him? What would have made it worth his while to drag the Institute's name through the mud?

I dialed Handelman's home number, which I knew by heart. His wife picked up on the second ring.

"Hello?"

I heard voices in the background, the clink of glasses, a dinner party.

"Miriam, it's Solomon."

A pause.

"Yes, Solomon."

"I'd like to speak for a moment with Joseph, if I may."

She paused again, Handelman's pug-faced wife, who had always bent over backward to be kind to me.

"I'm sorry, Solomon, but we're in the middle of dinner. Can he get back to you?"

I inhaled sharply. The air stung my nostrils.

"It'll only take a moment—"

"I'm sorry," she said firmly, and in a single instant I

understood that the curtain had fallen. Overnight, I had turned into a person whose phone calls do not get returned and whose name conjures shudders and pity. I tightened my grip on the bottle of scotch, and fought an urge to break its neck against the edge of my desk. (Although I didn't know it then, Handelman would eventually talk to me again. Just a few years later, he would telephone in the middle of his own divorce to declare his remorse and ask for my help. Which I gave, allowing me to return, however unofficially, into the analytic fold.)

I gazed at the burgundy velvet couch where a dozen patients had lain every day, and wondered if it would be forever tainted by my afternoon with Katrina. A small photograph of Freud, taken by a colleague in London, 1938, was propped, in a black-laquered frame, on a lower shelf of my bookcase. As my tongue snaked into my patient's mouth, the photograph might have fallen to the floor, glass shattering— but it didn't. In truth, Freud might not even have disapproved of my actions, certainly not as vehemently as my colleagues at the Institute. After all, he was the great-grandfather of countertransference. He didn't blab. He worked out his emotions in epistolary friendships, like the one with Ferenczi —not plastered all over the *New York Post*.

My feet carried me to the door. I had no idea where I was going. I rummaged for my house keys in the pockets of my jacket, which had fallen from the banister where I had flung it hours before. It lay in a heap, as if its wearer had shriveled to nothing.

"Dr. Grossman?"

"Whaaa—?" I nearly jumped out of my skin.

The nanny stood in the hallway, her white uniform glowing in the dark.

"Mrs. Grossman asked me to come and pick up a few things."

She carried two large lavender shopping bags from Bergdorf Goodman filled with toys and clothing.

My own hired help looked at me pityingly.

"She told me to tell you she wants to meet you tomorrow."

The nanny handed me a slip of paper, and I immediately recognized Ruthie's perfect Dalton script. *Leo's Coffee Shop*, 2 P.M.

The nanny and I left together. I closed the front door behind us, and we trudged down the steps, rounded the corner, and walked east toward Broadway without saying a word. There was a world between us, an entire universe of difference, and neither of us had the language, or the desire, to transcend it.

IT WAS SHORTLY BEFORE MIDNIGHT when I finally walked through Central Park to the Lenskis' townhouse on East Sixty-first Street—an ill-advised journey, no doubt. I was more than slightly drunk. I had wandered into several Irish pubs on Amsterdam Avenue—bars I had never even noticed before—and downed a few shots of whiskey. The balmy night air sobered me up. The park was empty, shimmering. The Indian summer grass blanketed its gentle hills. I entered at Seventy-second Street, just across from the Dakota, and strolled quickly, purposefully, hands thrust deep in my pockets. I could smell booze on my breath. I passed the lake on my left, inhaled in its mossy, dank late-summer smell and remembered taking Ruthie there during the spring, a month before Daniel was born. We had rented a rowboat and drifted around the lake's muddy edges as I sang to her like an Italian gondolier. Her belly rose and fell like its own separate being. My throat tightened with tears, but I fought them off. I had no business feeling sorry for myself. Anger, disgust, shame were all permissible. But self-pity? If I began, there would be no end to it.

"Katrina Volk, Katrina Volk!"

I spit out her name, shouted it into the empty, cavernous belly of the park. It echoed back to me, bounced weakly off the pavement. I looked up at the starry sky, the Big Dipper hanging there like a giant, inverted question mark. A child's paper airplane, caught in the leafy branches of a tree, suddenly dislodged and spiraled through the darkness. I picked it off the ground and carried it with me.

Lights burned brightly in the front parlor of the Lenski townhouse. I knew they couldn't see me as I lurked behind a lamppost, shivering incongruously in the warmth of the night. I breathed in deeply. The air smelled faintly of woodsmoke. I could see, in the soft glow of the parlor, the crackling orange light of a well-tended fire. Meyer and Mama were sitting on a loveseat, getting an early start on autumn, the backs of their heads clearly visible from the street.

My eyes drifted two stories up, to the suite of rooms where I imagined Ruthie, Daniel, and the nanny were camped out. I could make out a sliver of light beneath a shaded window. I knew Ruthie was behind that shade—

propped up in bed reading one of her paperbacks—and the baby was curled up in a crib nearby, lying on his side, safe in his Dr. Dentons. My heart expanded until it filled my whole body. I had a family! A family I loved! I knew each inch of Ruthie's skin as if it were my own. I could hear Daniel's breath whistling in my ears. I thought of them as my own right arm—taken for granted, to be sure, but utterly necessary to my survival and well-being. Surely the years it took to build that kind of intimacy could not be torn down in a single afternoon!

I lifted the brass knocker and let it fall with a dull clang. Once, twice. The outside lights clicked on, and I squinted in the brightness. Meyer's feet thudded to the door. His pupil shone against the peephole.

"Yes?"

"Meyer, it's Solomon."

"Do you realize what time it is?"

His voice was muffled through the heavy wooden door.

"I'll give you one minute to leave, Solomon, before I call the police."

I began pounding against the door. I pummeled with my fists, my feet, even my head. I was a battering ram, a beast. I wanted to be sure Ruthie heard me two flights up. I wanted each crack of my fist to be a nail of memory driven into Daniel's small, soft skull.

I walked away only when I saw the flashing red beacon of a police car turning onto Sixty-first Street from Fifth Avenue. I pulled up my jacket, bent my head, and shuffled off like an outcast, a criminal. I had entered a realm I had been bred for since birth: once again I had become the perennial outsider. Pitted against the great Meyer Lenski, I had no power. I was a pervert, an adulterer, a violator of several commandments and more than one oath. I felt the headlights of the police car shine against my back as I hailed a cab on the corner of Madison and headed back to Riverside Drive.

FIRST IT WAS JAIL I feared, Daniel. I knew if I violated even an iota of the restraining order Meyer eventually forced me to sign, I would wind up behind bars. It was not until years later—after Meyer's death—that I realized I had imprisoned myself with my own shame. I believed it was too late. Can you forgive me for that?

Never mind. Don't tell me your answer.

Will it mean anything to you if I tell you I spent two hours the following afternoon sitting in a booth at Leo's Coffee Shop, waiting for your mother? I drank two egg creams and three cups of coffee. She never showed up.

ELEVEN

I BOLT UPRIGHT in bed. Where am I? I shake my head hard. For a long second I am disoriented in this pastel luxury—the blond armoire, pale rugs, peach silk headboard, shadows of palm trees playing against the wallpaper. I focus on the sound which woke me up in the first place: an irregular bleating. I feel for my slippers on the floor, then pad into the living room, my life drifting back to me, as if I were remembering fragments of a dream.

My son is snoring, sound asleep, God bless him, on the pull-out couch. His face is slack, cheek pressed into a crisp white pillow, his mouth open, drooling, defenseless. A soft wool blanket is tucked just under his chin. I slowly lower myself into in a wing chair next to the patio doors, careful not to make a creak. Then, in the shadows cast by a bright California moon, I watch his chest rise and fall, and try to memorize his face. He is finer-featured than any other Grossman.

All the peasant blood has been bred out of him. He has the haggard, slightly neurasthenic look of a nineteenth-century scholar: delicate—almost feminine. His nose is Semitic, no doubt about that. His eyelashes are long, thick, lustrous—I'll bet they were Ruthie's favorite part of him. I can almost hear her crooning—*look at my boy, my beautiful boy*—

For the first time since beginning my odyssey, I am plagued with self-doubt. Perhaps I should never have made this trip. Perhaps I should have left my son alone with a half-hazy dream of a father brought to light through years of psychoanalysis: a shadow cast over his crib, a German lullaby hummed in the dark.

He stirs. I hold my breath, willing him to stay asleep. I feel blood churn through my system like high-octane gas in a rusty, beat-up car. I am sixty-four years old—not so old, really. Who knows? With any luck, I could be around, what, ten—even twenty—years. I feel something warm inflate my heart, a feeling as strange and distant as the touch of a woman. There is a shimmer to every object in this room, every burnished inch of it. For the first time in as long as I can remember, I have hope.

Daniel shifts and turns, stops snoring.

"Sorry, honey—" he mumbles.

His eyes flutter, then widen.

"Sorry!" he says again, awake, embarrassed. "What are you doing up?"

"I couldn't sleep," I croak.

"My snoring didn't wake you?"

He lifts his head off the pillow.

My throat tightens at the sound of his voice—so frail in

the middle of the night—I'm afraid I may break down weeping. I push myself out of my chair and head back to the bedroom. I am at a loss for words—the thirty years which have passed since the last time I watched my son sleeping seem thin as a membrane—as if I could reach a hand through the years and stroke his hot, round head.

"Sleep, Daniel. Sleep."

"Wait—stay with me."

The four most beautiful words in the English language.

"You want me to—?"

"Please"—he pats the edge of the couch—"sit for a minute."

Sleep has softened him; his hard edges have taken wing in the night. I pad over to the couch and lower myself gingerly, sitting so close that I can feel heat radiate from his body. It has been many years since I have felt such tenderness —for my patients I always maintain a certain professional reserve—as I tentatively reach out, push my hand through the membrane, and stroke his forehead, his dark silky hair.

He closes his eyes.

"Don't—"

I pull my hand back a fraction of an inch.

"I meant—don't stop," he whispers.

I sit quiet as a ghost, my hand smoothing Daniel's forehead as the digital clock blinks the hours away. I watch his peaceful, sleeping face become radiant as sunlight filters beneath the heavy curtains, and the stillness is replaced with chirping birds. My hand is thin, papery, ancient against his still-young cheek.

There is still time, my boy.

Two worn photographs lie on the coffee table next to the sofa bed. A thin shaft of early-morning light streams across them. The picture of Jenna is creased and bent around the edges. How many times has Daniel pulled it from his wallet and stroked his daughter's face as if it were a good-luck charm? A man with a child he never sees is an amputee. He walks through life with a limb missing, a chronic ache in its place. Does he think I don't know? That he calls that child's name in his sleep? That his wife, his marriage is more than a bad dream? Perhaps when he inspects plane crashes, he pays particular attention to the babies, silently renaming them: each burnt corpse curled into the fetal position is Jenna, Jenna.

My son's forehead is warm and smooth beneath my hand. I wish I were a healer—that I could melt away his pain with my touch, or better yet, transfer it into my own body where I could keep it contained with my own. I have spent my life trying, in the words of the great Sigmund, to reduce my patients' neurotic misery to common unhappiness. But when I look at my son, I know that I am the source of so much of his own neurotic misery—and nothing I can do will change that history.

I gently remove my hand, walk across the room and open the french doors. I want to roar, to shake my fist at the sky. The futility of my own life seems so huge that I can't imagine why I escaped wartime Berlin. Would it have made a difference if I had been gassed at Auschwitz? Yes, in fact, yes! Fewer people would have been hurt. There would have been no Daniel to carry the heavy bag of Grossman bones. Ruthie Lenski might have made a better choice. I look at the photograph of my granddaughter I have carried with me onto the patio. She is gorgeous, smiling a gummy smile, and in her dark brown eyes I see no burden.

I sink into a chaise longue, suddenly weak. With a sharp twig, I trace my initials into a terra-cotta tile. Maybe I should give some money to a charitable institution—UJA, or to the Holocaust Museum, perhaps—for a memorial plaque, an eternal candle dedicated in my name. *Solomon Grossman was here.* Never before have I felt the desire to leave my stamp on the world, like a dog lifting its leg to mark territory. While my colleagues wrote books and articles, I remained silent. What, after all, did I have to say about Freud's epistolary friendship with Ferenczi, Winnicott's playtime with children, Lacan's seven-minute hour? And if I did have anything to say—who would have taken me seriously? I felt lucky to even have a private practice, after the Institute debacle hit the papers. But I needn't have worried. Psychoanalysis is a private club, and its members protect their own: a trickle of referrals starting coming in, and eventually my practice thrived. But my personal life was another story. While my acquaintances spawned children and later, grandchildren—I wove an increasingly solitary web around myself, so dense and rooted it seemed simply to be a house I had built.

But now all that has changed. *Daniel. Jenna. Daniel. Jenna.* Their names are so beautiful I don't understand why the whole world isn't populated with Daniels and Jennas. Somewhere in Manhattan there is a little girl getting ready for kindergarten who sometimes has dreams she doesn't understand—dreams in a language she has never heard, in which she is running through deep brown forests—the dark forests of Hegel, Wagner, and Hitler. And here, right in the next room, is my beautiful boy—somehow alive and intact—with shoulders strong and wide enough to take his turn balancing the weight of the world.

"Good morning!"

Daniel steps through the french doors. He is wearing striped pajama bottoms and a tee-shirt, a white terry-cloth robe thrown over his shoulders. He yawns and rubs his eyes, blinking in the harsh sunlight. Behind him, a waiter in a tan uniform carries a room service tray laden with fresh fruit, a pot of coffee, a basket of croissants and muffins.

"Here you are." The waiter arranges our breakfast on a wrought-iron table, then cranks open the yellow canvas umbrella at its center.

"Will that be all?"

"Yes, thank you," says Daniel. He signs the check, then pours my coffee, grabs the plastic wrap off the top of my orange juice, and arranges the butter and jam around my plate.

"Usually I just have some cereal," I murmur, embarrassed by the fuss.

"If you'd like cereal I can call—"

"No, I didn't mean—"

"Really, it's no trouble." Daniel starts to rise from his chair.

He can't do enough for me.

"Daniel, please! Sit down! I just meant—this is all"—I wave my arms around us at the bougainvillea dripping over the sides of our patio—"I'm not used to this."

He takes a bite of a croissant.

"Well, get used to it!"

"But how can you afford—?"

"Think about it," he responds slowly. "My grandparents are both dead. And when my mother died—"

I keep forgetting that my son is rich. Serious, big-time rich.

"You inherited all of Meyer's money?" I ask.

"Most of it," he says matter-of-factly. "Actually, I can't touch the principal until I'm forty-five."

"Forty-five!" I exclaim.

"Keeps me out of trouble," he laughs.

"But—surely you don't need to work for a living—?"

"I don't work because I have to."

"Then why—?"

"You mean, what's a guy like me doing sniffing around plane crashes? I should have been on the partner track at some fancy law firm by now, or setting up the family foundation—"

"I'm not judging you, Daniel," I say mildly.

Of the many fantasies I entertained over the years, it never occurred to me that my son might investigate plane wrecks—and yet, when I saw him on television surrounded by smoldering metal, I didn't question it for a moment. Occasionally I imagined he might be a lawyer, even a doctor—though not, God forbid, a psychoanalyst. But once I discovered what Daniel had chosen to do with his life, it made perfect sense. Everyone in my life has gone off in search of wrecks: Daniel, Katrina. And Ruthie? Well, Ruthie chose me.

"It's pretty simple, really—they came to Yale, recruiting."

"Who?"

"The Air Force—"

"*You* joined the service?"

"They told me I would learn to fly jets," he says with a wry smile. "That was an appealing notion."

"And did you?"

"Fly jets? Yeah, I flew jets."

"What did your mother think of all this?"

A disdainful shrug.

My God, Ruthie must have been horrified! What a brilliant piece of rebellion my son concocted. One of the best I've ever heard in a lifetime of listening to patients' rebellions. I feel like reaching over and shaking his hand in congratulations.

"I needed to get away—" he continues.

"You could have taken a vacation!"

"No—what I mean is, I needed discipline. I was getting blurry around the edges—" Daniel says as he flicks away an ant crawling near the strawberry jam. "I was a mess by the time I was halfway through Yale. Drinking, taking—" He trails off.

Is he afraid drugs will shock me? Doesn't he realize I've spent a lifetime impassively listening to young patients tell me about the pills they pop, the powder they put up their noses?

"Anyway, during the summer of my junior year I decided to go to Officer Candidate School in Pensacola. So when I graduated college I became a first lieutenant and then went to flight school."

It's hard for me to fathom. I try to reconcile the young

man sitting in a hotel bathrobe in front of me with uniforms, glinting buttons, stiff salutes—

"I don't understand. So why aren't you an Air Force officer? Captain Gross? What are you doing working for the NTSB?"

"I don't think I would ever have lasted in the Air Force if I hadn't become fascinated with accident investigation," says Daniel. "I became safety officer of my squadron, and when I left the service I moved to the L.A. field office of the NTSB and became an air safety investigator."

"Ah, so that was 'graduate school,'" I say with some disappointment.

Why is it so important to me that my son have a string of initials after his name? What has a Ph.D. ever given me in the way of happiness?

"No, actually I got a degree from USC," says Daniel, "a Master of Science in Safety."

I never knew such a thing existed. Imagine being able to master safety.

"That's when I met McCall," says Daniel. "We got married. And then I was transferred to Washington."

"Why?"

"I guess I was a bit of a star," he says with no discernible pride. "I was good, a very good investigator—and Washington is where all the action is. The feds are responsible for all the catastrophic air carrier accidents that have any national significance—"

"And McCall?"

I don't want to push too hard. Everything in its own

time—but time seems to be moving fast, faster, like a slide projector gone berserk, flashes of images shooting by so quickly I can't possibly capture them.

"She didn't want to move, but we didn't have much choice. Washington was calling, and she was already pregnant with Jenna. We were head-over-heels with each other—"

He stops abruptly.

"Look, do we have to talk about this?"

"Whatever you want," I say.

"It's just a really sore subject."

"I can imagine—" I say lightly, pouring more coffee.

A few minutes pass in silence, punctuated only by the clink of china, the scraping of butter knives. Daniel doesn't speak again until the bread basket is empty. Then he leans back and folds his arms across his chest.

"What about you?"

"What *about* me?"

My heart skips a beat.

"We've now discussed my education, career, marriage, divorce—I'm sick of talking about myself. I want to hear about you."

His voice has taken on an edge which has already become familiar to me. He has quite an emotional range, this son of mine. The self-possessed young man speaking to me now bears little resemblance to the boy whose head I stroked through the middle of the night.

"Where should I begin?" I ask.

It is not a rhetorical question. I am at a loss, suddenly mute. How to explain myself? The narrative of my life twists in front of me like the winding two-lane highways of the

Southern California coast—*Falling Rock Zone*—full of hidden curves and danger. Do I begin in the Rykestrasse? With wartime Berlin? My immigrant teenage years? My marriage to Ruthie? Or perhaps this long last chapter—a thirty-year coda which begins and ends with the boy sitting in front of me. Will it make any sense to him if I say *my life stopped when you were a year old?* It would be the truth, more or less. Sure, there were women after Ruthie. A few months here, a few weeks there. Dinner dates who shared with me the sanitized versions of their own life stories. But I was never able to form a lasting attachment. After all, what self-respecting woman could go to bed with me under the watchful eyes of my ex-wife's wedding portrait?

A knock at the door.

"I thought I hung the *Do Not Disturb* sign," mutters Daniel as he heads into the suite.

I close my eyes and tilt my face toward the sun. My robe falls open, my pale hairy legs exposed to the elements for the first time in many years. I am suddenly tempted to throw off my robe and gallop naked along the manicured paths of the Bel Air Hotel, skinny-dip in the oval-shaped pool, nude-sunbathe in the hot morning light.

When Ruthie and I were here on our honeymoon, we snuck into the pool for a midnight dip, swinging our legs over the low, locked gate. We shed our terry robes at the pool's edge, our pale, goose-bumped flesh iridescent in the darkness. The pool was lit and was an eerie turquoise blue; steam rose into the night air. I remember Ruthie was so afraid someone might see us, she kept swimming lap after lap, back and forth, as if staying in motion would somehow make her less naked.

When I grabbed her from behind and tried to engage in a little aquatic activity, she pushed me away, laughing her lovely, cultured laugh, and led me back to our room, where we made love on the carpet, in front of the fireplace.

A shadow passes over my eyes, and I squint open. Daniel has been standing there for God knows how long, watching me, his head tilted. This is what we do to each other now: we watch when we don't know the other is looking.

"Penny for your thoughts," he says.

"Oh, they're worth more than that," I murmur.

Daniel tears open a large Federal Express package, revealing a brown leather book. On closer inspection, it appears to be a photo album.

"What's this?"

"I had it FedEx'd from Washington," says Daniel. "A friend of mine, Debra, is staying in my apartment—I called and asked her to get it to me."

He keeps it tucked under his arm, as if I might snatch it away.

"Ah, Debra," I say.

"She said she got a weird phone call from some guy on an airplane the other day. That wasn't you, by any chance, was it?"

I smile and flush.

"I thought so," he says. "Checking up on me?"

"Trying to."

A family passes by, just on the other side of our patio. The shrieks of fighting children pierce the sedate quiet; Daniel and I avoid each other's eyes until they pass. The sound is somehow embarrassing to both of us.

"So who's Debra?" I ask casually.

"She's just a friend."

"And she's staying in your apartment?"

"Yeah."

"Just while you're away—or do you live together?"

He turns away from me and shakes his head as if trying to clear it. His brow knots with tension.

"Listen—is any of this your business? You're asking me questions like you have a right to the answers—like you paid my college tuition or something."

Muteness pours over me like a syrup. After all, what can I say? The kid's right.

"Look—it's been years since I've spent more than an hour at a time with anyone. I don't always know how to behave," I break the silence.

"Debra is someone I see occasionally. McCall and Jenna," he says, struggling, "are the biggest losses of my life. I don't like to dredge all that up—I don't want to—I'm not sure I can."

"We don't have to talk about this," I say, not quite meaning it. "Let's just relax, take a swim—"

"I used to drink so much I blacked out," Daniel says haltingly, "and when I went into a blackout, all bets were off. I'd wake up sometimes with cuts on my body, bruises—and have no idea how I hurt myself."

He stops as abruptly as he started, closes his eyes tightly against the images. A small black bird alights on our breakfast table, pecking at crumbs.

"Go on," I say.

"I was like another person when I was drunk. It was

like I was stumbling through a veil and entering a parallel universe—a dark universe—where this other Daniel Gross would emerge."

"And what did he do that was so terrible, this Daniel Gross?" I ask gently.

He winces.

"He brought another woman into his wife's bed while their infant daughter was asleep down the hall."

Steady, Solomon.

If he were a patient, I wouldn't so much as blink. My expression would remain impassive. I might nod slightly, hands clasped in my lap. I would watch and wait. I might even clear my throat, probe slightly. Instead, I am lost. History has reared its ugly head, and I am powerless against it. If my son had been raised under my roof, no doubt he would have staged a rebellion against me, making his mistakes as different from mine as possible. Instead, it seems he has been destined to repeat the sins of his father.

"I'm sorry," I say.

"McCall walked in on us," he says. "We were passed out."

He is looking right at me, but I have the sense he isn't seeing me at all: perhaps a rumpled bed, a trail of clothes across the floor, a strange woman's arm thrown over his chest, a cottony feeling in his mouth, and then, instead of an alarm clock—a scream cutting the early morning, a shriek as old as time—*Get out! Get the fuck out of here!*—and the knowledge leaking into his heart that these words were not meant for the stranger in his bed, but for him.

"I couldn't even remember the woman's name," he murmurs.

"It might be better that way," I respond.

Katrina, Katrina.

"We tried, after that—mostly for Jenna's sake. We went to see a therapist. But there was no point, really. McCall couldn't forgive me."

I am flooded with memories of Ruthie. All my life I have wondered what would have happened if Meyer hadn't interfered—if she had kept our date at Leo's Coffee Shop. I like to think I could have regained her trust—but how hard would I really have tried? Perhaps she would have made it past the grief; but would I have made it past the guilt, given half the chance? Could I have lived each day looking into her hurt, accusing eyes?

"You probably think I'm a scumbag now," says Daniel.

"If you're a scumbag, what does that make me?" I blurt.

"What does that mean?"

"Nothing—" I stutter. "Only that I also abandoned my child."

"But Grandpa Lenski forced you—"

"I could have found a way," I say bitterly. "Meyer didn't rule the world."

"He certainly thought he did."

A small voice in my head tells me to come clean with my son. It might help him to know the truth about Ruthie and me. Maybe he'd whip himself less harshly if he knew. If he keeps this up, his shoulders will stoop beneath the weight of his own self-flagellation. Somehow I survived, but I am petrified, dried up as the sagebrush along the sides of the patio, and as battered by the elements.

I look around for something, anything, to do. Ruthie performs a perfect knife dive through my consciousness, slicing into the dark waters of my memory. She surfaces, slick and gleaming. I feel a pounding in my head, a great expanse calling my name, a swirling blue vortex.

"Let's go to the ocean," I say.

"Why don't we just walk over to the pool—"

"Pools are everywhere! There are pools in New York—" He hesitates.

"Are you sure you're up to it?"

"Why not?"

"Today's going to be a scorcher."

"So what's a little heat? We're in Southern California! Come on, Daniel. Let's live a little!"

His face breaks into a grin, years dropping away. I can picture him as a Bar Mitzvah boy sneaking behind the Sunday School to smoke his first cigarette.

"I'll call room service and ask them to make us a picnic basket. We can drive to Santa Monica."

THREE TIMES YOU BEGAN to ask me about my life, and each time we were saved by the bell, room service, a knock on the door. You never pushed too far. Perhaps you sensed that the few things I had already told you were white lies, sins of omission. Did you think, Daniel, that we'd both be better off if we didn't nudge the ancient encyclopedia of my history off its dusty shelf? Surely, as a detective, *you knew that information never disappears, only mutates. The truth is available, if you keep gnawing away at it. If you ferret it out like pieces of a wreck.*

THE PACIFIC is as calm as a lake. In the distance, whitecaps sparkle in the bright, noonday sun. Where is everybody? It seems Daniel and I have this paradise all to ourselves. On the other side of the low stone wall separating the beach from Ocean Avenue, pastel Art Deco buildings jut into the cloudless sky like gentle cliffs. To our left, a boardwalk extends into the ocean; a lone jogger runs to the end, then back again, his neon shorts bobbing like a kite. A flock of gulls gathers under the pier, pecking at some garbage left there.

"There's no shade," says Daniel, squinting.

He stops a dozen yards from the shoreline and lowers his canvas tote, which is bulging with the hotel's version of a brown-bag lunch: nestled into a white linen napkin is a chilled bottle of chardonnay, a baguette, a wedge of Brie, niçoise olives, and a small tin of fois gras—what are they trying to do, kill us with cholesterol?

Daniel is wearing a pair of baggy khaki shorts and a teeshirt which he peels off, revealing a pale sinewy chest. I once had that tough little physique—more of a runner than a fighter. Now, I unbutton my own shirt and slowly ease out of it, thankful for the genetic gift of a fast metabolism. In a certain sense, I have not aged badly—my muscles have not atrophied to nothing. But my chest has not been exposed to sunlight in God knows how long. I'm as pale as the underbelly of a sea creature, the inside of a shell. My skin is actually pearly, an unnatural white, covered with gray curls of chest hair.

At least I remembered to pack a pair of bathing trunks, such as they are. Lily Pulitzer, circa 1960-something. Green whales swimming across a pink background. I am wearing them now, though they are so old I'm afraid the elastic will disintegrate as soon as I wade into the ocean. Maybe the green whales will float away.

I spread out a towel, then lower myself to the sand, my stomach folding slightly over the top of my suit. What would have been the point of joining a gym, doing sit-ups all these years? For what?

"Hey, cool bathing suit," teases Daniel.

I don't tell him his mother bought it for me.

He plunks down, then rummages through the tote bag for sunglasses. When he turns to me, I see myself reflected in his mirrored lenses, my white hair puffed up like a cloud against the sky.

"Okay, so we're at the beach," he says.

I smile at him weakly. The twenty-minute drive, the five-minute walk from the parking lot have taken a lot out of me. I don't want him to see how exhausted I am.

"Hungry?"

"I feel like I just had breakfast," I say.

"I'll be back," he says, then jumps up and runs to the water's edge. I watch him, trying only to feel the joy of watching him. As he begins to run along the shoreline in the direction of the Malibu cliffs, he becomes younger and younger in my mind's eye until I can almost feel him, a chubby toddler, arms wrapped around my chest as we bob together in the waves.

My eyes sting. The sun beats against my stomach, blisters the tip of my nose. I raise myself up onto my elbows and look around. A sailboat glides in the distance, a catamaran.

A familiar pain stabs through my head.

"Daniel!" I call, frightened.

My voice gets lost over the ocean.

"Daniel!" I call again.

He bends down, picks something off the sand, then turns around and begins to jog back.

"Hey! Hey, Dad, look at this!" he says excitedly, then stops dead in his tracks and stares at me. It's the first time he's called me Dad. Has he ever said the word in his life? Perhaps one of his stepfathers insisted?

"I'd like to think you've never called anyone else 'Dad'—" I say thickly.

"I haven't."

He stands in front of me, panting. A strong breeze blows his hair across his forehead. He opens his hand and bends down to me, a perfect starfish nestled in his palm.

"Say it again."

"What?"

"You know."

"Dad."

"Again."

"Dad, Dad, Dad," he says softly.

I wrap my arms around him and we rock together as if swayed by the wind.

"That is so beautiful," I whisper roughly in his ear,

holding him tight. "The most beautiful word in the English language."

The throbbing pain grows worse. I grit my teeth into a smile. I brace myself against it as it crashes over me in a single wave. The worse it gets, the harder I wrestle it to the ground.

A lone gull soars over our heads, then lands a few feet from us, cocking its head at the contents of the tote bag, Brie ripening in the sun.

I push myself to my feet.

"I'm a bird," I flap my arms up and down like the gull, fingers fluttering. "I'm a birdie, and I'm flying!"

Daniel stares at me.

"Tweet, tweet!" I crow.

Never in my life did I dream it might be possible. I am soaring right into the center of the pain. Straight through to the other side.

"Tweet, tweet!"

I crane my neck, let my head fall back, and look at the sky, nearly losing my balance.

"Watch it!" Daniel yells, doubled over with laughter.

A jet roars by on its descent to LAX, leaving a smudge of pink in its wake.

I smile at my son, forearms still hovering by my sides, fingers fluttering.

"Don't you want to play with me?" I ask.

I want to turn back the clock, push the sun to the center of the sky, and keep it there. I want to go back to the beginning—*tweet, tweet, Danny, look—you're a little bird flying through the air!*—and watch his two-year-old face dissolve into giggles. I can almost feel the weight of his legs wrapped around my neck, his hands, the size of small plums, grasping mine. The magnitude of what I have missed is a physical blow that freezes my fingers in mid-air, stills my tapping feet.

I am a bird plummeting through the air.

"Come on," I say, suddenly frail. "The water's beautiful. Let's take a dip."

Daniel and I walk to the ocean's edge and beyond it, wading straight into the blue. The water is only slightly cooler than the air. He holds on to me as we slide down to our chins. I lower myself until my head is completely under water, keeping my eyes closed against the stinging salt. I fill my mouth with water—now I am a whale—and emerge slowly, pursing my lips and spouting a stream of water at Daniel's face.

He raises his hands to shield himself, laughing.

"Stop!"

I do it again.

"Stop it or else!"

"Or else *what?*" I taunt, splashing him with my hands.

He dives down and spits a whole mouthful of water at me. I don't protect myself as it hits me squarely in the eye—just watch as if through a rain-splattered windshield as Daniel becomes a child again, grateful that he cannot see the tears mixed in with the water dribbling down my cheeks.

"Okay, now are you satisfied?" he grins.

I nod, hit by a wave of inextricable sadness I don't want him to see. I came to California looking for something—I wanted the gift of Daniel, wrapped in a silver ribbon. Instead, I understand that it is I who have something to give him. If there's any legacy I can leave Daniel, it's the belief that he was able to cut through layers of my sadness like the inner rings of a tree, and—if only for this brief moment—make his father happy. If he truly believes he was able to do that, perhaps guilt will not erode his heart for the next thirty years, the way it has eaten away at mine.

"Happy?" he asks, reading my mind.

"Ecstatic," I say through a veil of melancholy.

He glows at his own triumph.

"Wait right here—don't move a muscle—" he says, wading to the shore. "I brought my camera—"

I sigh and watch as he sprints to our towels. The backs of his heels are raw and blistered—I should take him to buy a new pair of shoes—and his khakis cling to his backside.

"Hey, Daniel!" I call, but he can't hear me.

He rummages through the tote bag and pulls out the camera. His ribs stick out like piano keys; he could stand to gain a little weight. I hear him humming—how is it possible? —and then I realize it is not a human voice I am hearing, but the strains of a violin.

A hand reaches into my chest and gently, with great care, closes over my heart. I do not even have time to shout. My chin lowers into the whitecaps, then my mouth, my nose.

"Here we go!" calls Daniel as he races back into the water, splashing.

"Here we go!" he repeats.

But I am gone.

EPILOGUE

THROUGH THE BLUE I see you wavering, as if on the other

side of a fun house mirror. Your mouth opens and closes like a
gill. You dive toward me, hook your hand beneath my armpits, and
pull me from the water. Oh no, oh God no—you scream, holding
my head in your lap. But the music is beautiful, like a Schumann
lullaby. I see the notes, black ants marching across a white sheet
of paper. I hear the music all the way back to its inception, the
sequence of chords which once appeared to the composer in a
dream. The music has a shape—it draws itself across the sky—but
I am unable to digest it. I spit hard, it is impossibly bitter, but
nothing happens. My mouth doesn't move.

Your lips close over my own. You pinch my nostrils together,
blow into my throat, which is as lifeless as the thin rubber of a
balloon. You're going to fill me up with your own breath, puff me full
of air. You lean your head against my chest, already growing cold.

I hear the rhythmic beating of a drum. Or perhaps it is the

pounding of your heart which seems to fill the air all around us. I see the valves of your heart, the aorta, blood the color of aged red wine. You will live a long time, Daniel. You pull me to a sitting position, holding my face in your hands, and let out a wail which begins in your bowels and snakes up your throat. Tears roll down your cheeks, and I feel the sting as I watch you from above, from below, so close I can see the pores on your face.

You carry me in your arms like a bride. Pull a cellular phone out of your tote bag and dial 911.

"An emergency, Santa Monica beach across from the Shangri-La Hotel—my father's had a heart attack—"

You squeeze your eyes shut.

"I don't think so—he's not conscious—"

"My name is Daniel Gross," he says. "Daniel Grossman."

OUR BROWN-BAGGED LUNCHES lie abandoned on the sand like a meal that might have been left unfinished by an entire family fleeing Berlin in the night, half-eaten steaks still glistening on Grandmother's china. A sparrow chirps and I peer into its open beak, down to its heart the size of a small pebble. There is life all around us—throbbing, beating, pulsing. A spider spins its web against a low stone wall; a lizard slithers up a car tire; a married couple walks the pier, arguing. I can see clear through the wife's dress, her plain cotton underwear and cottage-cheese thighs.

You kneel beside my body and run your fingers along my shoulder, across my bare chest, tracing the stubble of my jaw. You place two fingers over my eyes, gently closing my lids.

Why—you are thinking—why him, why now?

At least we had this time, I call to you and watch with astonishment as my voice carries itself along the midday breeze and becomes your own thought.

So this is how it works! All our lives, parents try to control our children's hearts and minds—and then we die. In our deaths, we are able to hurl opinions, our most heartfelt sentiments, straight into our children's psyches—no wonder psychoanalysis is an impossibility: all my professional life, I was competing with the dead.

The paramedics race down the beach. A walkie-talkie squawks, and the stretcher gets stuck in the sand. The younger paramedic has a picture of his kid in his wallet—looks to be half-Asian. A gorgeous little girl with black bangs cut straight across her forehead.

"Outta the way, sir—" one of them says, waving you back.

He presses two fingers against my neck, feeling for a pulse. Can't he just tell from touching my skin? I have been watching myself turn the blue-gray of a deep-water fish.

"No pulse."

He pauses.

"Relative of yours?"

"My father."

There is no inflection in your voice. It is as flat as the sand along the edge of the ocean, not a ripple of emotion on its surface. Your training has kicked into gear.

"Ah, gee, I'm so sorry, buddy. Sorry."

You reach out your hands, palms up, entreating.

"What, what now?"

"We'll call the coroner and they'll send someone over to collect the—remains . . ."

The paramedic is thinking about dinner. His wife promised him spaghetti and meatballs, and his daughter is waiting by the door, listening for the crunch of his truck's wheels in the driveway.

"I want my father brought back to New York," you suddenly say. "His home is there."

"You can arrange that with the appropriate authorities."

"You mean—you can't take him with you now?"

"We only deal with medical emergencies."

You watch, cracking your knuckles, as they carry the stretcher out, empty.

Stop cracking your knuckles.

Your hands float to your sides.

You drape a towel over me. First you pull it all the way over my head, then you hesitate for a moment, bringing it back down and tucking it beneath my chin. You sit next to me, staring at my face. You are thinking that Jenna has my chin. Stubborn, determined, elegant with its small cleft—and you are hit by an inextricable wave of longing for her. It is a feeling I remember well—a cold emptiness.

A mother sparrow has made her nest on the other side of the wall, in the fragile crook of a tree. She sits regally on five—no, six—small blue eggs. Inside, there are embryos, the beginnings of hearts, beaks, feathers. Her round black eyes dart right, left, taking in the salamander slithering across the gutter. In the scattered clouds which have begun to pock the sky there is condensation, moist like a rolling fog. Tomorrow there will be rain.

You have left my side, and are now rummaging through the tote bag, looking for a corkscrew, bottle of white wine in hand.

You hold the bottle for a moment, squinting at the label, puzzled. How did this bottle wind up in your hand? Are you about to have your first drink in three years? Your mind is a war zone, shards of memory fighting each other. You see Ruthie standing on the porch in Greenwich, smiling carefully, her temples still black-and-blue from her recent face-lift; Ruthie's Jaguar bisected by a tree on the Saw Mill River Parkway; the cockpit of a fighter jet, controls as familiar to you as the speedometer of a car; McCall's pale blond eyelashes against a white pillow; and finally, Jenna's pudgy legs climbing you like a jungle gym.

It is the image of Jenna that makes you put down the bottle. But I'd like to think it might also have something to do with the metal garbage can I blow to its side, clattering against the concrete of the parking lot.

"What was that?" you mutter out loud, putting down the bottle. You eye it, shaking your head hard as if to get rid of the thought. If you're going to drink, it's not going to be a chilled bottle of chardonnay.

A series of numbers flashes through your mind—a Manhattan area code. You pick up your cellphone and dial. Blond eyelashes on a white pillow, the shriek of a little girl's voice—Daddy!

An answering machine.

"You have reached 555-1260," responds a brittle voice. "Please leave a message at the beep."

"McCall?—McCall are you there? If you're there, please, please pick up."

On the other end of the phone's wire, across a network of arteries crisscrossing the country like the veins in a human body, a lovely woman, no longer terribly young, stands in the dining nook of an Upper West Side apartment, one bare foot tapping against the parquet floor. Her knuckles are white around the white receiver, and all color has drained from her face.

"Mommy!" a little girl comes dashing down the hall, grabbing the hem of her mother's blue cotton skirt. "Telephone!"

"I know, sweetheart," McCall says quietly. "Ssshh. Let Mommy think."

"Who's on the telephone?" Jenna persists, her stubborn Grossman chin jutting out.

"No one, Jenna," McCall says more sharply as she picks up the phone. "Go watch Barney."

Barney? Who the hell is Barney? I watch as Jenna trounces off to her bedroom, where a purple creature named Barney has taken over the television. This creature helps Jenna forget the sadness she sees shooting from her mother's spine, or the way her mother sometimes seems to want her to just go away. What I would have given, just for a single second, to wrap my arms around that little girl! To whisper into the top of her head. Imagine—my granddaughter, with hair so blond it reflects the late-afternoon light streaming in through her nursery window! A mobile of pastel bunnies and birds floats above her head—a gift from Grandma Ruthie before she died. Inside Jenna, there are ghosts of all the women she might become; her veins are like paths—which way will she go? When we are born there is not one single, well-lit route to our adult selves—but rather, a series of footpaths through the wilderness of our souls, on which we can become hopelessly lost, or find our way through the forest.

My granddaughter's eyes are dark brown. She claps her hands together and squeals with delight. Does she know she misses her father—that some day she will feel a thirst for him which will parch her lips and desiccate every waking moment?

"What do you want, Daniel?" McCall asks, the phone wire wrapped around her hand like a bandage.

"Something's happened—" you choke. "I know you won't believe this, but—"

"Try me."

She is brittle, my ex-daughter-in-law. And who can blame her? From where I sit, it is impossible not to have compassion—for you, McCall, little Jenna—you're all just groping through the darkness.

"My father showed up."

"Your father? Is this some sort of joke? Isn't he—"

"He was alive. But now he's dead. And I—"

"Daniel, you're not making any sense. You're not plastered again, are you?"

"McCall, listen to me. I haven't had a drink in three years." You glance at the wine bottle and say a quick prayer. "I know this is kind of crazy, but—I need your help. Please. I'm standing on the beach in Santa Monica with my father's body. And I'm coming to New York to bury him."

All the sharp retorts in the world run through McCall's head.
She doesn't know whether to believe you. But something inside her softens.

"I don't understand—" her voice quavers. "He just appeared out of nowhere?"

"Yes," you say wearily.

"My God—" she says. "How are you handling this, Danny?"

You close your eyes.

"Not very well."

"What do you need?"

"Could you call and make funeral arrangements?" you ask.

"Of course. Where?"

"At Riverside, I guess."

So Meyer and I will once more be in the same place, though at different times. Ironies abound, even on the other side.

"I also need to pull some strings—to transport him—"

"Danny—" McCall shakes her head at what she's about to say, not even sure she means it. "Do you want me to come out there?"

"No need."

Silence. Breathing into receivers on opposite coasts.

"What was he like?" McCall asks softly.

"Sorry?"

"Your father. What was he like?"

Your shoulders begin to shake.

"He—" you sob. "He was—"

"Ssshh. It's okay."

"I never knew him—but I fell in love with him in a minute," you whisper. "I think I loved him all my life."

Jenna comes flouncing back into the breakfast nook.

"Mommy—" she whines more insistently.

"Is that Jenna?"

"Yes."

"Could I just—say hello to her?"

McCall pauses.

"I don't think that's such a good idea."

I settle over McCall's tense shoulders like a cloak of warmth. Give the guy a break, I whisper. But she isn't my own daughter, so she can't hear me.

"Okay," you say quietly. "McCall?"

"Yes?"

"I don't know how to thank you."

On the other side of the country, she places the receiver back on its hook. On Broadway, the evening rush hour is at its peak. Buses lumber uptown packed with office workers on their way home. An ambulance fights its way through traffic, siren wailing. It is headed for Mount Sinai—inside is a pregnant woman who is miscarrying. She writhes and moans, a pool of blood between her legs. Does she know—it is better to lose her baby now, than once it has a shape and a name? I see the tiny spirit leaving, floating beneath the crack in the back doors of the ambulance and disappearing into a cloud of exhaust fumes.

THE AIR on the beach is dense with spirits. One hundred and thirty-eight phantoms crumbling in the sand, drifting into the clouds, foaming along the surface of the ocean. You should only know—the victims of World Air 103 are crowded all around you, filling the sky like a flock of gulls. I search the air for a sign; how do we recognize each other, here in the blue? The rules have changed. I feel something move through me—a small, thrilling jolt—and wonder: It might be Meyer, or Ruthie, or even the late great Otto Grossman! There's no way to know for sure.

You are on the phone, making arrangements, calling in favors. A plane has been chartered to fly my body back to New York. Such laborious maneuvers, all to transport a lifeless piece of flesh! For all I care, you could toss me into the ocean, use me as whale bait. I watch as the coroner's men zip my stiffening limbs into a body bag. A small crowd has gathered on the pier, huddled together, watching.

You walk behind my body, head bowed. You are going through the motions, hanging on by a thread. A limo to the airport, a private jet. I always wanted to fly in such style—never did I suspect I would be zipped into a body bag and laid out in the aisle like an ice sculpture at a Bar Mitzvah. In the meantime, McCall has been busy —buying flowers, picking out a fancy casket, true shiksa that she is. She calls the New York Times and phones in my obituary. My poor patients—they'll read that their analyst has died while sipping tomorrow morning's coffee.

It will take more than six hours to make a trip I can now travel in a single breath. You slump down in the leather seat, strapped in like a good soldier. You stare out the window as the plane takes off, hand cupped around a glass of expensive water. You watch the urban landscape of Los Angeles blend into the green depths of the Pacific as the jet banks, then begins its flight across the country.

You sleep, a blanket pulled up to your chin. Your head rests against a small pillow wedged into the window, damp from the tears you cry in your dreams. Your mouth is slightly open, lips as soft as a little boy's. You are dreaming in Technicolor fragments—your mother's face, pale as the moon, her broken body pulled from the wreckage. In your dream she rises like a marionette and dances with me. We are two ruined human beings, Ruthie and I, but our dance has all the grace of an eighteenth-century waltz. As we dance together, her belly grows—it pushes against me like a watermelon in the sun until it bursts as you stir in your sleep, blinking open for a single unseeing moment, haunted, panting.

Oh, to be dead and to be an analyst! I can see straight into your unconscious, undiluted by lay interpretations made in the safe light of morning. Just when I no longer have dreams of my own, I can see yours from the darkened movie theater of the other side.

Call McCall, I whisper into your sleeping ear.

You stir, eyelids fluttering.

Call McCall and ask her to come to my funeral.

You check your watch, pick up the Airfone, and dial not McCall, but your own apartment in Washington. You live so simply, considering your endless supply of cash. A third-floor walk-up in an elegant Georgetown mansion. The phone rings next to a handsome sleigh bed. It takes me a moment to realize I am looking at my own marital bed—carted away from Riverside Drive by Ruthie's movers three decades ago. Did she use it for her other marriages? Put it in storage? It pleases me to think you have been sleeping in my bed all these years, my dreams hovering around you like ghosts.

A shape stirs beneath a heavy duvet, a graceful arm gropes for the phone, a mane of jet-black hair.

"Hello?" Her lips are puffed with sleep.

"Debra, it's me."

"What time is it?"

"About eleven—I thought you might still be up."

"I can barely hear you, Danny—"

"I'm on a plane."

"What's wrong?"

You were going to ask her to take the early Metroliner to New York and meet you at Riverside Chapel. You were going to try to explain to her that your father, once believed dead, turned out to be alive—but is now dead, really. Your spine curves with exhaustion even thinking about it. You consider Debra: sexy, undemanding, on the road more often than not.

You falter.

"No, I—"

"What is it, baby?" she yawns.

"Nothing. I'll talk to you later."

"Daniel, wait a second—"

You hang up, run a hand lightly over your eyes.

Call McCall.

You dial the New York number. McCall is in the shower, steam fogging the mirror, the small window overlooking the fire escape. She is listening to Glenn Gould play the Goldberg Variations on

WQXR. She doesn't hear the phone ring, but Jenna—go answer the phone, quick, quick, my little pumpkin, I breathe into her ear—Jenna jumps out of bed and runs down the long corridor and into the kitchen where she climbs onto a stool so she can reach the receiver, seconds before the answering machine can pick up.

"Hello?"

You inhale sharply. Her sweet little voice pierces your throat, and for a moment you cannot speak.

"Jenna?"

"Yes?"

What can you possibly say to her? You are overcome by paralysis. I know the feeling coursing through you as well as if it were my own.

"Hi, sweetie—" you choke.

"Who's this?" she demands, her voice like the upper register of a flute.

"A very good friend of your mommy's."

The shower has stopped. McCall furiously towels her hair, then slaps baby powder under her arms and between her legs. She opens the bathroom door, steam billowing into the hall.

"What's your name?" Jenna asks.

"Daniel."

"Where are you?"

"Right now? Believe it or not, I'm in the sky! I'm on an airplane—"

"Jenna?" McCall yells from down the hall. "What are you doing?"

"Talking to an airplane!" Jenna crows proudly.

McCall races into the kitchen and grabs the phone from Jenna's hand. Her towel falls to the floor. She is a glistening ode to modern toiletries, my beautiful ex-daughter-in-law. Powder and cream mix with droplets of water still running down her spine.

"Hello?"

"McCall?"

"How could you?" she asks quietly.

"Jenna answered the phone—I didn't tell her anything—"

"Excuse me for a moment," McCall says, then puts a hand over the receiver.

"Jenna, go back to bed, honey," she says.

"But, Mommy!"

Jenna crosses her arms over her chest, Grossman-style.

"Just do as I say, Jenna." McCall crouches so they're eye-to-eye. "Mommy needs you to go to your room."

My granddaughter leaves the kitchen and closes the swinging doors behind her, then hides on the other side, listening through the slats.

"You have no idea," McCall says into the phone, measuring each word, "how hard I've tried to make it okay for her that she doesn't have a father."

"I'm sorry," you say. "I needed to reach you. It's eleven-thirty at night in New York—I never thought Jenna would pick up the phone.

McCall considers this for a moment.

"What did you tell her?"

"Nothing. Believe me, I'm not trying to complicate things."

"How unlike you."

You take a deep breath.

"You said you would help."

"I am helping. I spent the whole night making arrangements. The funeral is at one o'clock tomorrow at Riverside Chapel. The *Times* is running an obit—"

"Will you come?"

McCall's eyebrows arch. She flicks a drop of water off her nose. The last time she saw you was at Ruthie's funeral. She thinks about that day—how she stood next to you, holding Jenna, as Ruthie's casket was lowered into the ground. Is she destined to see you only at funerals?

"Please, McCall. I know it's a lot to ask."

"Okay," she says. "I'll come—but not with Jenna."

On the other side of the swinging doors, Jenna cocks her head like a puppy at the mention of her own name. In her heart there is a hole the size of a pinprick. My ex-daughter-in-law has done a good job of mothering her. But in the absence of a father that hole will grow and eventually her insides will be hollow. Hey, bubeleh—I breathe into my granddaughter's ear—just remember you have a daddy who loves you.

McCall hangs up the phone, gathers the towel around her, and quickly opens the kitchen doors, finding Jenna huddled there.

"Where's my daddy?" Jenna demands.

Atta girl, my little chickadee.

"What do you mean?" gulps McCall. She knows she can't lie to a five-year-old. That kids have finely honed bullshit detectors.

"I want to know where's my daddy?" Jenna repeats.

"Sweetheart, what makes you ask me that now?" McCall plays for time.

"Was that him on the phone?" Her voice grows higher with each word.

McCall sits next to Jenna on the floor. Their hair is the exact color of wheat. Thin streams of moonlight angle through the skylight, capturing dust in the air. McCall grabs one of Jenna's tiny feet and holds it as if it were a hand.

"Yes, Jenna," she says slowly, "that was your father on the phone."

"Why didn't he say so?" wails Jenna. The tip of her nose has turned pink.

McCall closes her eyes. She is praying, though she doesn't believe in God. Praying to do the right thing.

"Believe it or not, your father didn't say so because of how much he loves you."

"That doesn't make sense! He doesn't love me!"

"Yes he does. And so do I."

McCall scoops Jenna into her arms and holds tight. In the wall behind her, a mouse the size of a thumb scurries through the floorboards, flipping over electrical wire like an acrobat. In the kitchen, cockroaches stealthily invade a box of granola like soldiers on a secret mission.

McCall rocks back and forth, her daughter's tears wet against her collarbone. She remembers breast-feeding Jenna, the way you would sometimes look in wonderment at the two of them across the bedroom in Washington. She knew you couldn't believe you actually had a wife and child. And finally, your disbelief turned sharp and cut into the very fabric of them. She is thinking—how to minimize the damage? Will it do Jenna more harm to see her father or to know he was only a few blocks away?

"I know you're really upset that you spoke to your daddy without knowing it was him," she says softly.

Jenna nods hard.

"Well, tell you what. How would you like to see him?"

Jenna turns to look at her mother, eyes shining.

"He's here?"

"He will be."

"When?"

"I'll have to arrange it, honey. Maybe even tomorrow."

"Oh, please, please, please, Mommy!"

Jenna clamors off McCall's lap and jumps up and down in the hallway. She is pure joy in pajamas, my new little Grossman, and as she spins her pirouettes I blow strands of hair from her forehead. Your mother's right—I whisper—your daddy loves you. Just wait, my precious. You'll see how much.

McCall remains slumped against the wall, unmoving. She wonders whether she's done the right thing, and who can blame her? The man she left—well, to be honest, she and Jenna were better off without him. But people can turn themselves around, change. You're just now reaching the age I was when I screwed it all up. You have a whole second chance—a "do-over," as Jenna might say. Look at me— thirty years of paralysis, and still, I managed to do one thing right at the very end. It may not have saved me—but perhaps it has saved you, Daniel. And that is all I could have possibly asked for.

IN THE AISLE of the Learjet, you are kneeling by my body and reciting the Mourner's Kaddish, stumbling through it, getting half the words wrong. Hasn't anyone ever told you Jews don't kneel before anyone—not even God? Yiskadal v'yiskadash—words you learned phonetically in a Greenwich, Connecticut, Hebrew school. I settle myself around you, resting in the creases of your closed eyes, and then

I realize—you are doing this for me. If I could cry I would. You think this is what I would have wanted, my dear, sweet boy.

"Sir?" the stewardess pokes her head through a curtained partition. "We're going to be landing soon, so if you'd take your seat?"

She thought she had seen it all, this flight attendant—rock stars and groupies, orgies in the air—but this is a first. She thinks you're cute, even thinks about slipping you her phone number—but she'll keep her hands off you if I have anything to say about it. I have bigger plans. There's a little girl in New York who is sitting by her bedroom window, watching each man who walks by on the sidewalk fourteen stories below, counting the minutes, waiting.

I AM IN A LOFT. An enormous, glaringly white space, with three arched windows overlooking a sun-flooded street. I zoom in on the street sign: the corner of Wooster and Broome. Two twisted metal chairs and a brown leather couch sit on an old Turkish rug in the center of the vast room like an island in the middle of an uncharted sea. Who could live in such fashionable emptiness? I spy a bluish light flowing from beneath a closed door and I float into the light, straight into the blue-black darkroom of Katrina Volk.

Her hands are pressed into a shallow basin, holding down the edges of a developing photograph. Her subject matter hasn't changed much over the years—the image is the aftermath of an uptown murder, the chalk outline of a body incongruous against the drooping daffodils of Park Avenue. A doorman's hat has fallen near the outline, the whole area sectioned off with bright yellow police tape: crime scene. There is no aesthetic justice—Katrina has aged gracefully. Her face seems to have deepened with time, her features sharper, more defined. Her hair, still long, is caught in a clip on top of her head, loose strands falling around her eyes as she squints into the basin. Her hands are another story, chapped and weathered by the chemicals they soak in every day.

She listens to music as she works. Today it is Vladimir Horowitz's romantic interpretation of Chopin's "Revolutionary Étude." Her eyes are the same deep blue of her youth, so piercing for a moment I can imagine she can see me swirling in the fumes. Such power I once gave Katrina! But now, as I watch her bones glow in this inner sanctum of hers, I wish her no harm. The corkboard walls are covered by her photographs. I scan them looking for a sign of myself—a photograph, a yellowed clipping. There is no such artifact. Who could live at the center of such destruction? This small, dark, private place away from the sheer uncluttered whiteness of her loft is the locus of Katrina's deepest truth. I peer into her mind as I once tried so desperately to do—and see it has been faultily wired from the start, corroded like an old battery. In the gray ooze I see her SS officer father marching, his shoes shiny as the eyes of bugs, stomping a well-worn path across her unconscious.

All my life I vowed that if I ever saw Katrina again, I would find a way to destroy her, as she destroyed me. But now that I'm wafting through the air around her, all I keep whispering is this: I forgive you, Katrina Volk. As God is my witness, I forgive you.

THE JET SCREECHES to a halt at Butler Aviation terminal at La Guardia. A hearse and town car are waiting. It looks like you and I will finally be traveling separately. The back door of the town car opens and a pair of slim legs in a proper black skirt swing to the ground as McCall unfolds herself and stands alone in the wind whipping off the tarmac, watching you descend.

At first you don't see her. You are carefully climbing down the steep stairs, grasping the rails, legs shaking. You force yourself to focus on one step at a time. If you think beyond the next minute you will become paralyzed, unable to go on. You remember this is why you used to drink a half-bottle of gin a night—this pain so great it cried out for anesthesia. You look up at the sky and see the thin gray streak a jet has left in its wake. You think, for a moment, that there is writing across the sky. That God is trying to speak to you. A tear rolls down your cheek, but you make no effort to brush it away. You are wearing your grief like a sign—an honorable discharge from the world of normal people going about their business.

"Danny!" McCall calls. "Over here!"

You finally see her.

"Oh, my God—" you whisper.

You start walking over to McCall, then break into a run. She leans against the side of the car, watching you—the new hollows in your face, the shadow of dark stubble, your pigeon-toed gait. You stop in front of her, reaching out two hands as if offering her something, then break down sobbing as she wraps her arms around you. She cups your head against her shoulder, keeping your back to the jet as three men carry the heavy plastic bag containing my body down the steps and gently load it in the hearse. She watches with tears in her eyes, this graceful young woman I never had the pleasure of meeting.

"You came—" Your cries are muffled into her shoulder.

"What, Danny?"

"You came—I never expected you to come—"

"Of course I came."

She opens the car door.

"Come on," she says softly.

You climb into the back of the town car together. A handsome couple, if I do say so myself. I can picture you growing old together, maybe even giving Jenna a brother or sister. In the way your bodies curve into each other I see a familiarity that has not gone away in the three years you've been apart.

Glad to be of service, Daniel. I'll tell you—it's easier to be a matchmaker when you have a little perspective.

In the back of the town car is an early edition of the New York Times. You flip to the back of the last section and skim the obituaries.

"Where is it?" you ask.

"What?"

"His obit?"

She sighs.

"They didn't run it. I don't know why—"

"But I don't understand—"

McCall wonders if she should tell you now. That the woman who answered the phone at the Institute had never heard of Solomon Grossman, and that a Nexus computer search, conducted by a journalist friend, had yielded some rather unpleasant news. She inspects your profile, so much cleaner and more chiseled now, after three years without booze. She decides to wait, to let you find out for yourself—or not.

"I want to stop by his house first—before the funeral," you say.

"Whatever you want."

You grasp McCall's hand and turn it over, tracing her palm. She pulls it away.

"Except me, Daniel," she says with dignity. "I'm here for you today. That's all. No one should have to do what you're doing alone."

You close your eyes and lean back.

"Exactly where on Riverside, sir?" the driver asks.

"Corner of Eighty-ninth," you answer.

Even the words are an effort. You want to go to sleep, McCall by your side, and wake up in about a week. Now that McCall is here, she is better than a Valium, a drink. You want to curl up in her lap and make it all go away. But then the car pulls up to the entrance of the brownstone where you spent the first year of your life. Will you remember anything—a flash of gray stone front stoop, ornate wrought-iron guard rails on the first-floor windows?

You ask the driver to wait, then stand uneasily on the sidewalk.

"This is it?" exclaims McCall. "He lived here?"

"Yes, why?"

"Jenna and I walk down this block nearly every day when I take her to the park—"

"Maybe you've seen him," you say.

"What did he look like?"

"Like any other old Jewish man around here," you say. "Tall, stooped-over, white-haired—" His eyes begin to well up.

You rummage through your pockets for my house keys, then walk slowly up the front steps of the brownstone—the same steps I used to carry you when you weighed no more than a bundle of groceries. Could I have imagined this, back when my mind tended to create whole narratives of drama and redemption? Could I have pictured my own son, shoulders stooped beneath the weight of my death, letting himself into the brownstone to have a look around?

"Come on," you call to McCall impatiently. "Come inside!"

You close the front door behind you, bolt it, then slide the safety chain. The hall is dark, illuminated only by two slivers of light from the rectangular windows on either side of the front door. You fumble for a light switch.

"Oh my God," breathes McCall after you finally find the

switch and the chandelier blazes overhead. You both blink, adjusting to the orange-yellow glare against the bone-colored walls which have not been painted in at least a decade.

She begins to walk down the hall.

"Oh my God—" she repeats.

"Stop saying that!" you mutter.

"But, Danny—come here—look at this!"

You walk to her side and look up at my gallery of photographs, unchanged in all these years. You reach for her hand and hold it tight. This time she does not pull away. Your palm is damp. You are seeing, for the first time, a picture of your parents on their wedding day. No doubt you have seen photos of Ruthie on her other wedding days—but you have never seen your mother and father together, much less a picture of me as a young man. Next to the wedding photo, a picture of you as an infant—remarkable only for the fact that it has hung in my hallway for thirty years.

"I can't deal with this—" you whisper. "I can't . . . McCall, please help—"

"What do you want me to do?" she asks.

"I don't know."

"Do you want to leave? We have a couple of hours before the funeral—"

"No, I just need to sit down."

The door to my office was left open a crack, probably by Mrs. Dodd, my able secretary. She is the only person who has ever had a set of keys to the brownstone—an insurance policy on my part to guarantee that I would not die and be left for weeks on end to rot.

You head for my office, tense and spooked. The creak of a floorboard makes McCall jump, then giggle nervously like a schoolgirl. The air is dank and still, a light film of dust covers the banister, the door frames. As you walk through my waiting room and into my inner sanctum, you breathe in sharply.

"I feel dizzy—" you murmur.

"Here. Sit on the couch—"

If houses had hearts, the ruby-colored velvet couch in my office would be mine. I spent my life focused on countless heads as they lay on the small embroidered pillow covered by a clean Kleenex—never allowing myself to even consider the possibility that one day you yourself might sit in this room.

"Look at all this." You shake your head.

"Do you remember anything?" McCall asks.

"Nothing. Not a thing," you say bitterly.

"You were only a year old—"

You scan the room: venetian blinds, slightly tattered desk, alphabetized bookcases, wooden file cabinets. You are trying to juxtapose those images with those of the childhood you do remember. How is it possible that the inhabitant of this dusty room was once married to your mother? You think of the house in Greenwich, lawns manicured as a golf course. Your heart swells with love for each of your parents—so human, so reckless, in their choice of each other.

Where to begin? You look at the file cabinets on the other side of the room with the methodical mind of an investigator—accustomed to sifting through wreckage far more complicated than that of a single life.

"What are you doing?" McCall asks as you push yourself off the couch and stride across the office, then open each file drawer, tossing each file unceremoniously to the floor in a cloud of dust.

"I'm not sure—" You sneeze.

"I don't think you should be doing this now—"

"Why not?"

"It's almost time—"

You thumb through stacks of manila files, all labeled carefully with patients' last names. You are looking for something unusual, out of the ordinary. You're operating on a hunch—hunches are your business. You must be very good at what you do. You have been in my house no more than a half-hour and already you are at the throbbing, beating locus of it all—the center of my life. If you had gone upstairs to my bedroom, you would have found little of interest. The bathroom medicine cabinet would have yielded no secrets. But my office files! It is as if you have stumbled upon the black box itself.

You zero in on a file labeled with your own initials, open it, and a cascade of baby pictures flutters to the floor, along with a lock of hair attached to a piece of Scotch tape, and I am embarrassed to say, a tiny white cotton sock.

"He kept everything—" you murmur.

"He must have really loved you," McCall says quietly.

"I can't believe this—" you say, weighing the sock in the palm of your hand.

A flash of memory bolts through your mind so rapidly you blink and it is gone: a mobile swaying overhead, a gray patch of light through an open door, the deep voice of a shadow looming over your crib. Hello, my chickadee.

"We really should go," McCall urges. She is starting to get worried. From the little research she did before your arrival, she knows the files are like land mines—that you're going to hit a trip wire any minute.

You ignore her as you thumb through file after file—more morbidly curious than anything else. Will you see the name of someone you know? Someone famous? How horrifying, that the lives of hundreds of people are reduced to a pile of paper on a dead man's floor.

"What's this?" You hold up the only unmarked file.

Bingo. With unerring radar, you have uncovered The File.

"Danny, not now—"

"Hold on a minute!"

You squint at the first clipping, so fragile it might disintegrate between your fingers before you're able to make sense of it.

"What the hell is this?"

You look at the accompanying photograph, then scan the article, your initial disbelief sinking by degrees, first into numbness, then horror. You are wading into the arctic sea of my history, step by step, word by tabloid word—and I cannot stop you. A physical pressure builds up all around me—a futility that seeps into my capacity to think. If the dead can feel pain I am feeling it—as I watch your face crumble with recognition as you begin to read aloud from the clipping, hands trembling.

"A 34-year-old psychologist, Solomon H. Grossman, has been suspended from his duties and clinical practice at the Institute after being accused by a female patient of sexual molestation—"

You trail off and look at McCall helplessly.

"Oh no," you say softly.

I'm sorry, Daniel.

You close your eyes for a moment, then abruptly dump the contents of the whole file to the floor. A handful of clippings, the note from Ruthie asking me to meet her at Leo's Coffee Shop, the separation agreement drawn up by Meyer's office, a copy of the order of protection Ruthie sought against me, our divorce decree, a few magazine photographs of Katrina—the file had become my catch-all over the years for everything painful. I figured if I kept it in one place it might hurt less. Never did I consider how easy I would be making it for you to dig up the dirt.

You pick up the order of protection and scan it, reading aloud again, your voice increasingly harsh.

"'. . . It is ordered that the above-named defendant, Solomon H. Grossman, observe the following conditions . . . do not harass, intimidate, threaten, or otherwise interfere with Ruth Lenski Grossman or members of the Lenski family or household . . .'"

"Damn it!" you explode.

"Danny!" McCall exclaims.

"Why did he lie to me? He told me how respected he was, how he was one of the best—"

"He could still have been one of the best," says McCall, bless her heart.

"He didn't give me a chance to really know him," you cry. "He was a lie!"

The pain intensifies. Not this. God not this. As long as you believe in the tenuous threads connecting us, we will be bound together. I will be able to see into your mind and help you in whatever way I can, a guardian angel perched on your shoulder. I will be able to protect you in death the way I couldn't in life. But if you begin to hate me—if the cold harsh feelings swimming around you right now solidify into a coat of armor—there will be nothing I can do. I will be cut loose—forced to fly off into the cosmos, to wherever they send unloved, unwanted souls.

"He was your father," says McCall. "That wasn't a lie."

"Yes—" you mumble, looking down at a magazine spread of Katrina Volk. "He certainly was my father."

You are fading. I look into your mind, your heart, and see it all becoming flat and murky. Inaccessible. I howl into your ear, but you feel only a gust of air, a draft, a chill shooting through you.

You check your watch and sigh.

"We'd better get going."

You glance around the office at the disarray, the piles of folders and papers. Don't you understand that I could never tolerate disorder around me because my inner life was in such chaos? That alphabetized bookcases went a long way toward soothing the frayed edges of my unconscious? There are so many things I wish I had told you. Now you will have to figure it all out for yourself—if you even want to. Maybe you'll just have the Salvation Army cart it all away—from the ruby velvet sofa to every last scrap of paper. The detritus of my life dispersed among urban homeless shelters—I can almost picture it.

You leave my office and walk into the corridor, but instead of opening the front door, you pause at the foot of the staircase. Another flash of memory, this time of these same stairs looming, creaking, as you, enveloped in soft, powdered arms, were carried up, up—to the huge feet in shiny black shoes waiting at the top of the landing. You remember the sound of screaming—adult voices, not your own infant shrieks—absorbed by the cushioned softness and baby blue walls of your nursery.

"Wait right here—" you say, bounding up the stairs.

"What are you doing?"

"I just want to see something," you call.

When you reach the second floor you stop to look around, eyes alert, sniffing like an animal. The hallway is dark, a small night-light flickering like a yahrzeit candle. I must have forgotten to turn it off. You do not touch the knob of my closed bedroom door. You move past the bathroom and continue down the hall until you stop in front of the door to what once was the nursery. There are more family photographs on the walls, but you don't pay attention. How is it possible? Your feet have guided you.

You open the door and swallow hard. The shape of the nursery, with its curved wall, light streaming in from the window overlooking the treetops of Riverside Park, is as familiar to you as your mother's womb—and as inaccessible. A few years after Ruthie left, I finally redecorated it, in a manner of speaking—gave the crib to Hadassah and the bassinet to the sisterhood of the local shul. I tried to make a den of it with a couch and television—but I could not bring myself to throw away the mobile which still swings overhead. I even left all the stuffed animals, which stay piled into one corner, a forgotten menagerie.

You crouch down to pick up a teddy bear and hold it to your chest, rocking back and forth like a little boy, weeping. You sit on the floor and tearfully look around the room, the mobile of wooden animals a totem of your dreams.

I blow into your ear with the little strength I have left. I breathe my spirit into you to do with what you will—and you shiver, thinking of your father, who lived alone in this house with nothing more than memories and shattered dreams, dozing in this room beneath the mobile, one eye open, waiting. The hours I spent in this room, daydreaming of you! You grew up in my mind, riding the jagged edge of my imagination.

You see it all in vivid color, a vision so bright you bury your head in your hands, the room swirling. You think of the father you knew for only a short time—the weathered lips spouting like a whale in the Pacific Ocean, hands fluttering like a bird's wings. I watch as your fury turns into something milder. Something tempered with compassion.

"Danny?" McCall pokes her head around the corner. "Are you all right?"

"Oh, sure," you laugh wearily.

She walks tentatively into the room and stands in front of you for a moment, studying you gravely. You are clutching a teddy bear to your chest, and are scrunched into a pile of stuffed animals in the corner of this musty room, wiping your tears on your shirt sleeve.

She offers you a hand and you walk down the stairs, past my gallery of photographs, past the landing where Ruthie first screamed the word divorce—and out the front door.

The driver is waiting, but you motion him to roll down the window.

"It's a beautiful day—we'll walk," you say.

As the car pulls away from the curb, McCall steers you across Riverside Drive and you both enter the park. There are only a few puffs of clouds in the bright blue sky. A perfect day for my funeral. Inches beneath the thawing earth, worms are tilling the soil and stalks of spring flowers are beginning to breathe. A squirrel is scurrying across the path and over the gnarled roots of the very same oak under which I ate my lunch for nearly forty years.

The playground is filled with shrieking children, slipping down sliding ponds, sifting through the sandbox. McCall shields her eyes as she squints into the distance, her heart thudding. It's the right time of day for Jenna to be here—and sure enough she hears Jenna's laugh before she sees her on the swing, coaxing her baby-sitter to push her higher.

Her daughter's hair whips around her face. Her blue-jeaned legs pump back and forth and her head is thrown back, her flushed cheeks to the sky. There is a white-haired man standing near the swing set, hands thrust deeply in his pockets. McCall notices him because he is carrying an old wooden sled—why would he be carrying a sled when there is no snow on the ground? She squints harder to try to make out his features, but he is gone.

"Look, Danny—" she whispers.

You follow her pointing finger.

"See anyone you know?" she asks.

You search the playground. A wind has picked up, scattering a few dead branches across the hill. You pass over each child's face until you see Jenna on the swing, her stubborn legs kicking higher than any of the others—and you look questioningly at McCall, who gives you a tight little smile and a shove.

"She's been expecting you," McCall says.

You begin to walk—then run—to the edge of the playground. Go on, my precious boy. Go on.

Make things right.

MODERN CLASSICS

☐ **THE ARMIES OF THE NIGHT** *History as a Novel/The Novel as History.* **Winner of the Pulitzer Prize and the National Book Award. by Norman Mailer.** The time is October 21, 1967. The place is Washington, D.C. Intellectuals and hippies, clergymen and cops, poets and army MPs, crowd the pages of this book in which facts are fused with techniques of fiction to create the nerve-end reality of experiential truth. (272793—$11.95)

☐ **THE THIRD POLICEMAN by Flann O'Brien.** Here is the most surreal, fantastic and imaginative murder comedy ever created, from one of Ireland's most celebrated authors. "Astonishingly inventive . . . to read Flann O'Brien for the first time is to be plunged into joy."—Bob Moore (259126—$12.95)

☐ **UNDER THE VOLCANO by Malcolm Lowry.** Set in Quahnahuac, Mexico, against the backdrop of conflicted Europe during the Spanish Civil War, it is a gripping novel of terror and of a man's compulsive alienation from the world and those who love him. "One of the towering novels of this century."—*The New York Times* (255953—$12.95)

☐ **1984 by George Orwell.** The world of **1984** is one in which eternal warfare is the price of bleak prosperity, in which the Party keeps itself in power by complete control over man's actions and his thoughts. As the lovers Winston Smith and Julia learn when they try to evade the Thought Police and join the underground opposition, the Party can smash the last impulse of love, the last flicker of individuality. (262933—$11.95)

☐ **ANSWERED PRAYERS by Truman Capote.** For years the celebrity set waited nervously for the publication of this scandalous exposé. For years, the public eagerly awaited its revelations. The narrator is P.B. Jones, a bisexual hustler. The heroine is Kate McCloud, the most desired woman in the jet-set world. Between them they see, do, and tell—everything. "A gift from an unbridled genius!"—*Los Angeles Times Book Review* (264839—$11.95)

Prices slightly higher in Canada.

Visa and Mastercard holders can order Plume, Meridian, and Dutton books by calling **1-800-253-6476.**
They are also available at your local bookstore. Allow 4-6 weeks for delivery.
This offer is subject to change without notice.

"Compelling!"   —*Vanity Fair*

"Exposing the mind of a devastated 64-year-old man is a courageous literary endeavor for a young female author, and *Picturing the Wreck* gives credence to the power of the imagination and to the writer's skill. With fluid prose and keen observation, Dani Shapiro takes us achingly close to the center of a tortured heart and soul."   —*People*

"Dani Shapiro is not reluctant to confront taboos . . . crossing boundaries between patient and therapist . . . shifting swiftly between past and present without sacrificing pacing or control. . . . She generates heat and light in illuminating her characters."
—*Washington Post Book World*

"Dani Shapiro interweaves personal and political history; tiny gold threads of possibility peek through, but no seams show."
—*Library Journal*

"Dani Shapiro is a master of the balancing act . . . moving effortlessly between life and death, sin and redemption. . . . The intimate destructions of marriage and the desperate loneliness of lost love are deftly portrayed in a prose that is at once spare and lyrical . . . testing the very limits of narrative and taking the story and our perceptions of its meaning to a whole new dimension . . . the dimension of forgiveness and love . . . delicate, almost ethereal."   —*Louisiana Times Picayune*

"Desperate love . . . convincing and moving . . . a triumph!"
—*Publishers Weekly*

"Guilt and the search for redemption . . . reminds us of the reason that novels are still being read and written—they can find a home in our hearts."   —Tim O'Brien

"Affecting . . . [Solomon's] pathos evokes shades of Graham Greene's 'whisky priest.' "   —*Atlanta Journal Constitution*

DANI SHAPIRO teaches creative writing at Columbia University and in the graduate program at New York University. She lives in New York City, where she writes and reviews for many magazines, and is working on a memoir.